Invasion!

A Crossover Worlds Novel

SUZAN HARDEN

This is a work of fiction. All characters, organizations and events in this novel are products of the author's imagination and are not to be construed as real. Any resemblance to persons, living or dead, is entirely coincidental.

INVASION! (A Crossover Worlds Novel)
Copyright 2023 by Suzan Harden
ISBN-13 - 978-1-64918-030-8

All rights reserved

Published by Angry Sheep Publishing
Findlay, Ohio

Cover Design by For the Muse Design
Interior Design by JW Manus

To all the writers who started with fan fiction

MORE BY SUZAN HARDEN
(Each series is in suggested reading order)

Crossover Worlds
Invasion!

Justice
Sword and Sorceress 28 ("Justice")
Sword and Sorceress 30 ("Diplomacy in the Dark")
Justice: The Beginning
A Question of Balance
A Modicum of Truth
A Matter of Death
A Touch of Mother
A Twist of Love
A Virtue of Child
A Hand of Father
A Measure of Knowledge
A Hint of Thief

The Justice Thalia Stories
Snowfall

Murder Most Fowl

The Sweetest Poison

A Granddaughter of Mine

Too Many Fish in the Sea

Tales of the Twelve
The Trickster Priestess and the Demon

Bloodlines

Blood Magick

Zombie Love

Zombie Confidential

Zombie Wedding

Amish, Vamps & Thieves

Blood Sacrifice

Love, War & a Bulldog

Zombie Goddess

Ravaged

Sacrificed

Reality Bites

Ghouls in the Grocery

Resurrected

Bloodlines Shorts Anthology

Bloodlines: The First Boxed Set

Seasons of Magick

Spring

Summer

Autumn

Winter

The Seasons of Magick Anthology

Millersburg Magick Mysteries

Spells and Sleuths

Fae and Felonies

Magick and Murder

888-555-HERO

Hero De Facto

Hero Ad Hoc

Hero De Novo

A Very Hero Christmas

Hero De Jure

Hero In Camera

Hero Amicus Curiae

A Very Hero Wedding

A Very Hero New Year

Hero Ad Litem

Queer Eye for the Super Guy

Soccer Moms of the Apocalypse

Pestilence in Pumpkin Spice

Famine in French Vanilla

War in White Chocolate

Death in Double Mocha

Miscellaneous

Sword and Sorceress 31 ("Pig-Headed")

Sword and Sorceress 32 ("Unexpected")

Practical Witches

Revenge Served Hot

The Yule Switch

Chocolate for Dinner

Silver Shoes and Pigs' Ears

Solar System Services, Inc.

Alone Is Not Lonely

For updates, news, and giveaways, join Suzan's mailing list or visit her website at www.suzanharden.com. You can also check her out on Facebook @SuzanHardenWriter.

CHAPTER 1

The Crimson Palace, Naha, the Kingdom of Ryukyu,
Year of the Twelve 1979

Anthea DiBalance, Chief Justice of the city of Orrin in the Queendom of Issura, ducked the slashing black talons of the demon who rushed her. Sweat stung her eyes as she whispered the words of her spell, charging her sword with Balance magic. Her backswing sliced into the demon's neck.

Its screech of fury and pain blended with the shouts and screams of the soldiers, wardens, and clergy around her as they engaged the demon army. Issuran, Jing, and Ryukyuan languages mixed in a cacophony punctuated by the chittering tongue of the invaders. The alien scent of their foes mixed with the coppery odor of human blood and the stink of the loosened bowels of the dead.

An arrow charged with Light magic whizzed by her head. The second demon wailed, a sound reminiscent of fingernails on slate. Both the demon and the arrow collapsed into a pile of ash.

Despite the first demon's efforts to increase its body density to trap her weapon, Anthea wrenched her sword free from its neck. From his perch on a street lantern, Brother Jian of the Jing Empire's Temple of Light launched another arrow into the third demon. Anthea charged her sword with magic once again as she danced backward from her own foe.

The demon's swing to disembowel her was slow and clumsy from the effects of her first spell. Since all demons were the darkest shade of black to her, thanks to her strange sight, its loss of coordination and lack of its normal speed were the only indications to her the demon was aging faster than normal.

Anthea thrust her sword into what passed for the demon's chest. Her foe crumpled to dust as her spell discharged through it. Despite their much longer lifespans, not even the demons could escape the ravages of time. And time was the domain of the Temple of Balance.

She panted and looked around her. Her heart tried to force its way up her throat. Ambassador Quan of Jing along with his wife Shi Hua and Sister Yin Li of the Temple of Love, had been backed against the abutment of the first bridge into the Crimson Palace.

Not Ambassador Quan any longer. With the assassination of his brother and nephews, he was now Crown Prince Bao Quan Po of the Jing Empire. If the Issuran and Jing escorts didn't keep him alive and get him home to be crowned emperor, Jing would fall into a civil war.

Then the demons would eat the leftovers.

The Ryukyuan guards didn't dare open the gates to the palace. Not even to save their own forces. Despite the palace's multiple gates and intricate moat system, the demons would overrun the palace guards in a matter of heartbeats. It rested on the clergy and their wardens to reinforce the soldiers and keep the demons' attention away from the civilians evacuating the rest of the city of Naha.

"Jonata!"

Her warden lit the flashbang in her hand and tossed it in the middle of a group of demons harassing High Brother Luc of Light and Yin Li's young son Yin Shang where they perched on the outer moat wall. The flashbang exploded. Luc used the demons' disorientation to fire Light-charged arrows at them. Within three heartbeats, the demons crumbled into dust.

"With me!" Anthea shouted. Her other warden Long Feather defended another Light priest who launched his own arrows from a seat in a cherry blossom tree. But where in Light was Warden Mateqai? He wouldn't have left Lady Shi Hua's side unless—

Anthea shove the ugly thought away. Now was not the time. Not when they needed to deal with the demons first, else more people would die.

Jonata drew her sword and the long knife she used for defense and raced after Anthea. Together, they killed two of the demons at the back of the pack threatening Quan, Shi Hua, and Yin Li.

The pack split, and the back half whirled and charged the two Issuran women. Anthea threw up a quick ward. She rocked back on her heels from the increased mass of the half dozen of their enemies slamming into her magical shield.

"Drop your ward, Justice!" Brother Jin yelled from behind her.

Anthea released her spell while she and Jonata backpedaled. More arrows charged with Light magic flew between them. Four of the demons crumbled into dust. Brother Fa of Wildling, in his second form of a gigantic feline called a tiger, ripped off the head of the fifth demon.

The sixth demon galloped on all fours toward the City of Naha's public gardens. Anthea raced after it. More sweat dripped into her eyes. She needed to kill it. Sundown was moments away, and then her fellow clergy would be at a huge disadvantage. She'd be the only one who could see in the darkness, and there was no possibility of defending the future emperor's entire party and the Ryukyuan company who had escorted them to the palace.

Ahead, a figure stepped from behind a blooming cherry blossom tree. The greenish-gray skin gave away its identity as much as the demon magic it wielded.

Skinwalker. A sorcerer who studied and apprenticed to the enemies of the human race. Using demon magic corrupted the person until they were no longer human.

It flung a spell at Anthea. She threw up a ward, but the impact knocked her on her buttocks. Jonata yanked Anthea to her feet, and the pair raced after the demon.

The skinwalker cast a second spell, but not at the women. Anthea gasped at the explosion of colors. It was quite literally a rip in reality. Bile surged up her throat. The demon raced for the tear in space and time.

"What in Balance—" However Jonata perceived the damage of the skinwalker's spell caused her to slow a heartbeat.

"Jian! Take out the skinwalker!" Anthea ordered as she raced past Jonata. She had to catch the demon before it reached the portal.

Light magic surged behind her. A shrill scream filled the air.

The rip flickered. Anthea lunged for the demon.

And found herself flailing in midair. No demon. No ground. No sky.

Then she fell.

CHAPTER 2

*Greenwich Village, the Island of Manhattan, New York,
the night before Samhain*

Shan Wong-Washington jerked awake at Cu Chulainn's low growl. The Irish foxhound lay at the foot of the brown comforter on hers and Jamal's wrought iron bed. Ambient light of New York City filtered past the closed blinds of the bedroom's only window and displayed the dog's alert posture.

"What's wrong, boy?" she whispered. Cu Chulainn jumped down from the bed.

Or rather stepped down. The dog was so huge her sister-in-law Tanja and cousin Livvy rode him when they were toddlers. He padded down the short hallway between the bedroom and the living room of the loft.

Shan slid out from under the covers. The hardwood floor was oddly cold against her bare soles, considering the building's cranky furnace had been blasting so much heat before bedtime she'd resorted to a sleep t-shirt and shorts instead of her sweats. She listened carefully, but there was only silence from the loft's living room. Were the girls up to something? Was that what riled Cu Chulainn?

The wolfhound wouldn't have growled if it were something minor. He would have trotted out to the living room and stopped whatever mischief the girls were up to.

Shan followed the dog out to the living room. The night light in the kitchen gleamed yellow, softening the harsher glow of Manhattan from the skylight.

No shenanigans here. Both girls were out cold. Tanja was curled in a tight ball, sound asleep. Only a few of her dark braids poked out from under her blanket. Livvy lay beside her, blond hair and limbs sprawled across the couch and chair cushions the girls had placed on the living room rug to form their bed. They had convinced their respective parents Shan needed the company while her husband Jamal trained at the Johnson Space Center. It definitely wasn't the two nine-year-olds who woke Cu Chulainn.

The wolfhound stood at the top of the narrow steps leading from the second-floor loft down to the store. Another low growl rumbled deep in his chest. Something was definitely wrong in the shop.

Shan had double-checked all the doors and windows of Morrigan's Cauldron, the store Jamal's mother co-owned. Everything had been locked, and the steel gates pulled into place and secured. As much as she loved Manhattan, and Greenwich Village especially, she wasn't stupid about safety. Especially not with two little girls under her care.

The wolfhound placed a paw on the first step, his hackles raised.

"No," Shan commanded in a whisper. "Stay."

Cu Chulainn gave her a look that obviously said he disagreed with her, but he did as she ordered.

Shan went back to the bedroom to slip on her canvas shoes. A slight hum came from the closet. Crap. If Lexi was indicating danger, things were worse than Shan feared.

She carefully slid open the closet door. The scabbard hung from its peg, and Lexi's hum became even more urgent.

Shan drew her husband's sword from its scabbard. The steel gave off a slight golden glow in the dim room. The blade had gone through many titles over the millennia. The Sword of Lugh. The Spear of Destiny. Excalibur. Now, the family simply referred to it as Jamal's crazy singing sword. Or Lexi.

And she was a much better weapon than Shan's aluminum baseball bat.

"Tone it down, girl," Shan whispered. "You're going to give us away to whatever is downstairs."

The sword's glow dimmed, and she stopped the eerie humming.

"Thank you." Shan retrieved her charmed copper knife and crept back out to the living room. The girls hadn't moved at all. Cu Chulainn remained on guard at the top of the stairwell.

Maybe she should call her mother-in-law Phylicia. As a witch, she could handle whatever was down there.

No, there was no sense waking up the in-laws if Shan was blowing something out of proportion.

A bang came from downstairs. Cu Chulainn growled low in his chest.

"What was that?" Livvy whispered.

Crap. Both girls sat on their makeshift bed, wide awake and staring at Shan.

Another crash resounded through the building.

"Lock yourselves in the bathroom, and call 9-1-1," Shan whispered. "Cu Chulainn, guard the girls."

The wolfhound still didn't look happy, but he padded over to Tanja and Livvy. He let the girls grab their phones before he herded them toward the bathroom.

Shan crept down the narrow steps, Lexi providing her the only light. While some of the objects Morrigan's Cauldron carried were expensive, a thief couldn't easily fence a one hundred-pound block of purple quartz. Phylicia took the receipts for the day for deposit on her way home. So, why the hell would anyone break into the store? Everyone in this neighborhood knew better than to mess with Phylicia. Or Grandmother Wong.

So it had to be someone desperate. Or whacked out on drugs. Or both.

Shan opened the door at the foot of the stairs and froze when the hinges creaked. She held her breath and listened. Someone shuffled around in the storefront. Whoever it was hadn't heard her. Thank goodness for old creaky buildings in the Village.

She carefully locked the door to the stairs and crept through the storeroom. The beaded curtain hung between her and the invader. Odd chittering came from the dark figure standing behind the cashwrap. The light from the street showed the gates over the door and windows closed. Had her potential thief jimmied the front door and its gate and closed them so the NYPD didn't get suspicious? Or had he come in through the back door? Were there others with him?

None of her conjectures made sense. Phylicia's wards would have deterred someone trying to come into the building after hours, as much as the locks and gates did.

The rustle of parchment came from the top of the cashwrap. For a split second, the figure mumbled words that sounded like the similar language spouted by the woman who had brought in a strange grimoire.

The customer claimed she found the volume in a dead aunt's attic and had wanted an appraisal. Of course, the woman came in after Phylicia had left for the day. Was someone trying to steal the grimoire?

Or worse, had the woman cast a spell inside the store without Shan realizing it to get the intruder past the after-hours wards?

The more she watched, the less the thing flipping through the grimoire resembled a human being. Its moves were jerky, and its joints seemed to move in unnatural directions. The smart thing would be to retreat to the loft stairwell, lock the door behind her, and wait for the cops. But between the locked gates and the warding, the thing was trapped inside the building with Shan, Cu Chulainn, and the girls.

And unless Shan unlocked the gates, there was no way for the police to enter Morrigan's Cauldron and apprehend the intruder.

Which still left the question of how the intruder got into the building in the first place.

None of her speculations mattered. An unannounced night visit wasn't good, and surprise was still on her side. She eased her left hand past the strands of beads and nudged the light switch.

The antique fixtures flared to life. The thing messing with the grimoire jerked. It was definitely not human. It was covered in grayish—well, the dermis wasn't exactly scales, but it wasn't skin either. And its limbs were tentacles tipped with wicked-looking talons.

One of the tentacles shot toward Shan, ripping off several strands from the bead curtain in the process as it tried to grab her. She deflected the appendage with Lexi. Both the sword and the intruder screeched. A thin trail of smoke curled from the blade. Even more smoke poured from the lengthy cut on the now-drooping tentacle.

Whatever the thing was, it was vulnerable to magic. Too bad she didn't have her grandmother's talents.

The intruder backed away from the cashwrap and began chirping and chittering, the noises reminiscent of locusts. The sounds were rhythmic. The damn thing was casting a spell.

Anger and protectiveness of her family fed Shan's strength, and she charged the creature. It dodged both the Tuathan blade and her blessed copper knife while dragging its disabled tentacle.

A swirling vortex of white and blue lights appeared behind the intruder. The tone of its speech changed. A fifth tentacle shot from its body and wrapped around her right ankle. Nausea raked her at the alien feeling of its epidermis.

Before she could bring Lexi down on the tentacle, the intruder yanked her off balance. Her hip landed hard on the polished wooden floorboards, but she managed to keep her hold on both the sword and knife.

The sounds changed again to chittering broken by huffs. Laughter. The damn thing was laughing at her. She knew it in her bones as the damn creature dragged her into the vortex with it.

CHAPTER 3

Allen George Memorial Park, Canyon Pointe, State of Mojave, the week before Christmas

Aisha Franklin-Garcia, the superhero known publicly as the Ghost Owl, winced as the talons of the creature she fought tore through her uniform, and worse into the skin of her thigh. Her hero togs were made out of material stronger and suppler than Kevlar, and her skin was damn near invulnerable. It meant the thing was as strong as she was. Not to mention, the cuts burned like hell.

She punched at what appeared to be the creature's head. Her fist went through the head as if it had phased its molecules like fellow superhero Shadowstar. But when she tried to pull back, her arm was stuck inside the creature.

Fine. Let's see how it handled supersonic speed. She flew straight up, dragging the creature with her. Her predecessor as the Ghost Owl had literally designed a variation of her suit for NASA. The repair systems had already ejected sealant along the rips, so she wouldn't have any issues as the atmosphere thinned. For all her powers, she still needed to breathe. The heads up display inside her helmet ticked off the altitude.

Something squeezed her chest. She looked down to find the creature's talons had disappeared. Tentacles had wrapped themselves around her body. Okay, maybe she did need to worry about breathing.

She flew even faster. This dang thing clinging to her body had to have some kind of oxygen or temperature limit. Above her, the sky darkened to deep blue as the atmosphere thinned.

At twenty miles above the earth's surface, the creature's tentacles loosened. Its entire body phased, and her arm slipped free of its head. The thing may be able to change its density, but gravity was still queen. It plummeted. Aisha dove after it.

Plasma flickered around the creature's body and Aisha's visor. The creature fell towards a thunderstorm developing east of Canyon Pointe. While Aisha's foe probably wouldn't hit anybody in the state park on the other side of Lake Del Oro from the city, she couldn't take the chance. Once again, she poured on speed. Static built along her suit in the unstable atmosphere.

Lightning erupted between her and the clouds below. Her suit was insulated from the electrical surge, but the bolt of lightning nailed the falling creature.

Aisha grinned to herself as the thing disintegrated in the one-point-twenty-one gigawatts of Mother Nature's power. One down. She needed to get back to Canyon Pointe. She headed west and flew as fast as she could. No doubt complaints would be filed with the city, county, and state governments for the sonic booms in her wake.

Inside Allen George Memorial Park, the Canyon Pointe police were trying to clear the area of civilians who were still on their feet. EMTs attempted to treat and evacuate the people who had been mauled by these things. It was up to Aisha to keep these creatures occupied and away from the population of the city until backup came.

Relief spread through her when Sparx's voice crackled through the speakers in Aisha's helmet. "What the hell are these things?"

"You got me," Aisha replied. "Don't let them get near you. I just got raked by their claws, and they drew blood. But the one I dealt with didn't like lightning much." She grabbed a couple of kids hiding behind a tree and delivered them to waiting officers without an additional word.

"Roger that." Sparx's crisp answer was almost drowned out by Nix's sonic shriek.

"Think Doctor Triassic has been experimenting again?" Aisha asked. "These things have a reptilian look, but they definitely aren't cold-blooded."

"Don't know, but whatever they are, they smell worse than the snake exhibit at the zoo," Sparx said.

Aisha's predecessor had also designed the suit to filter out toxins when she was breathing in normal earth atmosphere, so she didn't get a hint of whatever odor Sparx picked up.

"Guys, they don't like water either," Nix said. "I knocked one into the fountain, and I think it died."

Aisha's visor darkened as Sparx cut loose on a third creature now that the park was clear of civilians.

"How many are left?" Sparx asked.

Aisha rose a few feet above the grass and spun to scan the area. "I see two more by the pin oak grove." She flew in that direction.

And was horrified to see a civilian lying on the ground between the pair of creatures.

"Sparx!"

"Right behind you. You kick them away from the guy, and I'll blast them."

Aisha was fast enough the creatures didn't have a chance to phase. She literally kicked the one on the right straight up into the air, tearing out a great deal of green foliage as it arrowed skyward. Lightning flashed behind her. She reached for the other one, but it sliced its talons across the throat of the unconscious young man laying beneath the tree. A weird chittering cough sound erupted from the creature as she grabbed what appeared to be its throat.

Her suit's radiation alarms blared for a second before all the suit systems died. Aisha squinted at the blinding surge of blue and white light. The only thing she knew for sure was that she and the creature were falling, tumbling through empty space with no idea of which way was up.

CHAPTER 4

Otherwhere, Time – Irrelevant

Samantha Marie "Sam" Ridgeway St. James, the vampires' goddess of Death, locked the gate to her afterlife and trudged through the black sand of Otherwhere, a region between places no one but the gods traversed. Even then, none of the deities she personally knew took Otherwhere, or the things that hunted here, lightly.

She wasn't sure she liked being so busy lately. Even worse, she wasn't sure she liked being worshipped. It gave her a weird feeling. She'd never been the center of attention when she'd been alive. Now that she was dead, it was just plain uncomfortable. But when the dying called for her, she had to respond.

And very few of the dead were people she personally knew. Ares and Morrigan had ripped her new assholes for turning Duncan, Alex, and Connie into gods like her when the stupid, fucking dino demons had killed the three of them. But according to Sam's deity pals, the other pantheons would regard Sam making gods out of more of her dead loved ones as an act of war.

Ares and Morrigan would know as the patrons of War in each of their pantheons.

The warning came because Alex's death was technically the Incan god of Death Supay's fault. Alex made the mistake of promising Sam's Incan counterpart he'd hunt down the assholes who stole Supay's tumi, the symbol of his power. Which Alex accomplished, a few seconds before Sam engaged the dinosaur god trying to break into her home dimension, causing Mount Rainier to erupt.

Come to think of it, Puget Sound didn't look much better than Otherwhere these days.

The sepia sky in the between space looked bleaker than normal, and a sharp, arid breeze snapped her long black coat against her legs. In the distance, something howled. Something she didn't recognize as a denizen of Otherwhere. A chorus of familiar shrieks and screams answered the initial howl.

The birdcats hunted something, which wasn't a good sign.

She stopped and sniffed the air. The odor of something living penetrated the acrid scent of Otherwhere. Ginger mixed with something else. The second scent was vaguely familiar. She sniffed again. Not quite the smell of a dinosaur demon, but still slightly reptilian. But the ginger scent she definitely knew.

Now, why the hell would any witch be stupid enough to enter Otherwhere? Not even a god in their right mind would come here unless they were desperate. Only death resided here. A living soul would attract the undead predators who prowled this place, which explained the familiar shrieks and screams. And there were worse things than the birdcats in Otherwhere.

Sam took another deep breath. Along with the ginger came the smells of rotting jungle vegetation and—

She sniffed again. Chinese food? But underneath them all was the odor of fresh apples.

Humans. More than one.

Shit.

Sam ran in the direction of the living. Behind her came the skittering of chitinous feet on the diamond-sharp sand. She glanced behind her. Eyes glowed blue and orange amongst the ever changing shadows. Another pride of birdcats followed her.

Fuckity-fuck. If she didn't reach the humans first—

Well, watching someone's soul being eaten wasn't a pretty sight.

CHAPTER 5

Anthea tumbled across the ground and gained her feet. The substance she stood on shifted as if it were sand beneath her boot soles.

But it didn't look like normal sand. It glowed a dull red.

The demon, however, was black as always. She had a sense it was surprised. Maybe it didn't expect she'd followed it to here.

Wherever here was.

Anthea sent a quick prayer to the Twelve, pleading that this wasn't the demons' realm. If it were, she'd be dead and consumed in a matter of moments. And that's if she were lucky. The demon howled, but it wasn't hunger or rage or pain. It was something she'd never heard from one before.

Fear.

The demon took off running on all four limbs.

Anthea cocked her head. Now, why would it be fleeing from her if they were in its home dimension? Against her instincts, she took off after it, but the odd, glowing sand was as difficult to run in as normal sand was on the Peaceful Sea beaches or in the Valley of the Lost. If she was in the demons' domain, she needed to kill it before it called its fellows down on her head.

The dry, cold wind blew sharp grains in her face while she ran. Whining similar to an abused dog came from the demon. It loped up a dune toward what appeared to be a large clump of basalt. When Anthea reached the top of the dune, she squinted as something burning seared her sight. From the awful odor, tar surrounded the stand of rock and had been set aflame.

Movement on top of the rock caught her attention. Yellowish creatures watched her and the demon. They had a general feline appearance except the ruff of feathers surrounding their heads and covering their sinuous tails. And if she could see that much detail from this distance, the yellow felines must be bigger than the panthers of the Gray Mountains.

She half-ran, half-slid down the slope when something crashed into her back. She landed face-first in the odd sand, and her sword slipped from her grasp.

"What in the Twelve—" She spit several times to get the bits of sand and gravel out of her mouth.

"Drel roe alry wens?" someone asked.

Anthea rolled to a sitting position. A young woman stood over her, her hand outstretched to help her upright. A perfectly normal human woman.

Except she glowed slightly, and not from her body heat. There was a blue-white nimbus surrounding her.

The younger woman repeated her gibberish before her eyes widened. She leapt past Anthea. A sword appeared in her right hand and a copper knife in her left. She faced another demon.

Anthea's demon ran across a basalt bridge into what appeared to be the amphitheater formed by the rock outcrop. It was the only reason she knew this was a different demon. She clambered to her feet and grabbed her own sword.

The younger woman slashed at the demon. It ducked under her guard, but she expected the move and swept the copper knife across the demon's equivalent of a face. It let out a high-pitched shriek of pain and backed away.

How in Balance could a copper blade keep its edge? Copper may be fine for cups, coins, and jewelry, but it was normally useless as a weapon. The metal was too soft and malleable.

Anthea charged her sword with magic and jumped into the fray. The younger woman automatically sidestepped to keep the demon between them. She kept the second demon occupied long enough for Anthea to stab the creature in its back and discharge her spell. The mystery woman plunged her own sword into the demon.

Power erupted in a horrendous explosion, both psychic and physical. Anthea tried to raise her wards, but she found herself falling once again, her limbs flailing. Then all the air was forced from her lungs, and every single atom of her body screamed in pain.

CHAPTER 6

Shan blinked the stars from her eyes and tried to push to her feet, but her arms and legs refused to work. What the hell happened? That felt more like a conventional explosion rather than a spell.

A high-pitched cry came from nearby.

"Lexi?"

This time, the sound tolled in a lower octave, but it had a mournful note. Like the sword was in pain.

Oh shit! Panic forced Shan's limbs to move, if not exactly perfectly. She crawled on her belly across the sand over to Lexi. If she'd hurt Jamal's sword, he'd never forgive her. It had been Rain's last gift to him before she and Tom died.

Shan reached the sword. Half of the blade was covered with what felt like medical-grade silica gel, the kind doctors used in breast implants decades ago. Otherwise, the sword seemed to be intact.

"I'm so sorry, Lexi." She sat upright and pulled Lexi in her lap. Her sleep t-shirt and knit shorts were also coated with gel. And the said gel attracted every grain of sand it could hold. At least it didn't smell as bad as the stuff burning in the trench around the largest hunk of rock in this weird desert.

The goo had also splattered across the oddly warm sand, its epicenter where the creature that pulled Shan through the vortex had stood. It had landed on another person. Someone wearing a black hooded robe. The person who'd also been caught in the explosion when they both stabbed the creature.

Shan looked around wildly. A clump of black fabric with two black boots sticking out lay on the other side of the splatters. She climbed to her feet. Her legs shook, but she managed to stay upright.

Glitter caught her eye. Her knife. While the simple copper knife wasn't fancy or sentient like Jamal's singing sword, Rain had gifted it to Shan after she used it to destroy the *kiang shi* that stalked her and nearly killed her father.

She lifted the antique blade and winced. The tip had bent. It wouldn't take much to straighten it, but she feared the damage might have destroyed the spell Rain had placed on the knife. She threaded the drawstring of her sleep shorts through the loop at the top of the handle and knotted it. That would have to do for now to carry it.

Shan crossed to the unmoving form and rolled the body on its back. Or rather her back. The black hood slid away from a woman's face.

Her skin was a shade darker than Shan's while her intricately braided hair was glossy black. She had the full lips and sharp cheekbones of some Native American tribes, but her nose was almost Romanesque.

Shan knelt, laid Lexi beside her, and checked the woman's vitals. She breathed normally, and her heartbeat was steady. The explosion must have knocked her out.

Shan leaned back on her heels and examined their surroundings. A bloody sun rested just above the horizon. The sepia-toned sky sent a chill down her back. Grains of the weirdly warm sand coated her legs and shoes thanks to the gel. Odd black rocks rose in the distance, rocks very similar to the stone—no, not a stone. It wasn't an outcropping as she'd thought. A walkway of the same black rock spanned the burning stuff and led into an amphitheater. Diamonds paved its floor, and a ruby the size of a tank sat at the opposite end from the entrance. Where the hell had that creature brought her?

A groan drew her attention back to the other woman. She emitted a second groan before her eyelids fluttered open. The woman's irises and pupils were the same color as the setting sun.

Shan tried to stifle her gasp, but failed. A wry smile tilted the other woman's mouth. She spoke, but Shan didn't recognize the woman's language.

She shook her head and frowned. "I'm sorry. I don't understand."

The other woman gestured at her red eyes and spoke again. Maybe she understood the color of her irises and pupils was unusual.

Shan winced. "I'm sorry. I didn't mean to offend you."

The other woman chuckled. Maybe they didn't know each other's language, but they could get their points across to each other. The other woman rose on her elbows and looked curiously at the goo splattered over the sand. She asked a question.

Shan shrugged and mimicked an explosion with her hands. "It went KABOOM!"

The other woman said something else, most of which made no sense, but her sentence ended with a series of syllables that sounded like Mandarin.

"Shanguang peng," Shan repeated. "Flash bang?"

"Flash bang," the other woman repeated. She sat upright and mimed lighting a fuse and throwing the object. "Shanguang peng."

Did she think Shan had pitched an explosive at the creature, or was she saying she had? Shan repeated the other woman's motions and pointed at her.

The other woman shook her head and pointed at Shan. She shook her head and mimed thrusting blades into something and an explosion. The woman stared at Shan, her expression thoroughly confused.

Shan examined the area around them. Something glinted a few yards away. She pushed to her feet and strode over to retrieve the woman's sword.

When she picked it up, a weird sensation tickled her palm. Ignoring it, she brought the other sword back to where the woman sat before Shan picked up Lexi. A weird electric sensation sizzled along her nerves. Some instinct said the two swords should never touch. And she realized what had happened.

She simulated the two swords thrusting into the creature and yelled, "KABOOM!"

The other woman nodded. "Flash bang." She climbed to her feet and held out her hand towards her own sword. Her right eyebrow rose.

Shan reversed the blade and offered it to the other woman pommel first.

She smiled and accepted the returned sword before she found a clean spot on her robes and wiped the goo from her steel. After she sheathed her weapon in the scabbard strapped to her back, she motioned at Lexi.

Shan frowned. Did the woman want her to hand over Lexi? She didn't like the idea of being unarmed in this weird place. She especially wasn't going to lose Jamal's property.

The other woman flicked her left wrist. A small stiletto appeared in her fingers. She made an exaggerated motion of touching the small blade.

"Oh." Shan looked at Lexi. "Is it okay if she touches you?" Lexi sang a cheery note. Shan faced the woman. "Lexi is okay with you touching her."

The other woman seemed confused by the whole exchange, but she nodded before she replaced the stiletto in her wrist sheath. Shan held out Lexi, laying flat across both of her palms. The other woman tentatively touched the blade with her index finger—

She jerked her hand back at the same time Lexi let loose with a metallic squeal. Shan jumped backward, wanting to protect the sentient sword. However, the other woman stayed where she was and shook her hand like she'd received a nasty electric shock. Lexi cried the same high-pitched note she had after the creature exploded.

If Lexi was a magic sword made by the Tuatha de Danan, maybe the other woman had a power that reacted to the fae blade.

"Are you all right?" Shan lowered Lexi and stepped toward the woman, but the cloaked figure skipped back and drew her sword again. The last thing Shan wanted was a fight with someone she couldn't understand.

The red-eyed woman shouted something. She didn't sound angry. No, the strange syllables sounded more like a warning. She jabbed her free index finger at Shan.

No, not at her. Behind her. Shan whirled to find another creature like the exploded one running straight for them.

And a helmeted figure out of the science fiction B-movies Jamal loved pursued this creature.

By flying.

Without wings.

CHAPTER 7

Aisha landed hard on her left shoulder and tumbled across what felt like sun-heated sand. With her suit's systems down, the sealant ejectors and air supply weren't working. When she came to a rest on her back, she unlocked and shoved up her visor. Huge gulps of air eased the black spots across her vision, but the sky looked bizarre.

She blinked a few times while the ache in her chest eased. Nope, the sky really was sepia, not the blue of a winter afternoon in Canyon Pointe.

She rolled to her feet. Roughly ten yards away, the creature from the park looked around wildly at their surroundings. It shrieked and ran away from her on all four limbs.

Her blood burned. The little bastard had murdered that kid in the park. Sliced the young man's throat for the sheer joy of it. It wasn't getting away with such an evil act.

Aisha flicked the switch for the manual vents in her helmet, shoved her visor back in place, and launched herself into the air. Damn, that creature was fast. The way it ran and screeched, the thing was terrified.

Now, why would something that enjoyed killing be scared of her? Its fellows certainly weren't afraid of any of the supers who responded to the alarm at Allen George Memorial Park. Had it tried to teleport away? Had her suit interfered with its attempt to 'port? Had they ended up in some-place that was far more dangerous than the creature's home?

Or worse, was the damn thing running home to its mommy and daddy?

In any case, she needed the creature to get back to her own home, so she flew after it. A green dot blinked in the lower right corner of her visor. Her suit's computer was trying to reboot. Hopefully, the radiation burst hadn't corrupted the software, but she wasn't solely dependent on the suit like Tim Canyon, the first Ghost Owl.

The air was oddly chill compared to the warmth of the sand. Where the hell had the creature taken her? It raced towards an outcropping of black rock. No, not an outcropping. It was more like a small mountain. In the distance, more black rocks of various sizes poked out of the black sand. The creature wasn't running for the mini-mountain. It was running towards the two people standing roughly a couple of football fields from the—well, not a mountain. The huge thing was an open-air stadium. It looked like it had been grown instead of constructed. The interior floor of the structure was covered with a fortune in diamonds. She spotted what appeared to be enormous felines with feathers on their tails eating a creature on the ruby dais. A creature like the one she chased.

No wonder her opponent was terrified.

Aisha poured on the speed and tackled the creature before it reached the two humans. Claws penetrated her uniform and stabbed into her left calf. The hot sand rubbing against the cuts twisted the wounds into agony. How the heck did these things slice through her nearly impenetrable skin? Were they denizens from the Mayan underworld Xibalba like some of the other monsters that had attacked her and her family?

Grateful for the superpowers her mother-in-law Xquic granted her, Aisha swung both of her fists down on what appeared to be the creature's head. It phased to avoid its head getting crushed, which freed her leg. She rose into the air. The blinking dot in the corner of her visor switched from green to yellow, and the heads-up display flashed on.

Most of the weapons systems were down. Only the anesthetic pellet launchers worked and only on manual. They weren't the tasers, but they were better than nothing.

Aisha grinned to herself, lifted her right arm, and took aim at the creature. She pushed the release button. The pellet smashed into the creature's main trunk, sending the powder in every direction. The creature opened its mouth and sucked in the drug.

The murdering monster didn't shriek in pain, bellow its anger, or pass out despite Aisha's crossed toes. Instead, it sneezed. And continued sneezing like someone suffering from severe hayfever.

The sneezing fit shook the creature until its talons transformed into tentacles. The fleshy appendages shot toward Aisha and wrapped themselves around her wrists.

Static raised the small hairs all over her body. Had Qiang managed to follow her to wherever the hell she was? Was her suit's electronics shorting out? Or was the creature generating its own electric field like certain eels and the tentacles were dragging her closer to it in order to shock her to death?

"Get away from that thing!" the woman in shorts and a t-shirt yelled.

"I'm trying!" Aisha kicked at the trunk of the creature only to have her boot stick in its body. And the dang thing was still sneezing.

The woman in the black robes was screaming something incomprehensible, but the sparks arcing between her hands were all too familiar. And it was obvious she didn't have the same control over electromagnetism Qiang had.

The last thing Aisha wanted was to be electrocuted by a stranger in some alien place far from home.

She levitated and began spinning. Faster and faster. The shape-shifting creature screamed and released her. She dove for the woman in shorts and a t-short who carried a sword. Aisha slowed a bit in order not to break any of the other woman's bones when she grabbed the stranger before flying out of the range of the robed lady with the lightning powers.

Well, Aisha hoped she was out of range.

Light flashed. Her suit's internal computer and electrical systems crashed for a second time before the crack of thunder deafened her. The electrical discharge blew blinding sand. She gently landed and tried to shield the woman she carried as best she could from the sharp grit pummeling her supersuit. All she could do was pray the robed woman's own clothing protected her from her own powers.

Because the debris in the wind would have abraded even Aisha's impenetrable skin.

CHAPTER 8

The first explosion caused by the interaction of fae and witch magick didn't surprise Sam. But the bolt of lightning at ground level caught her off guard. The electrical blast's concussion knocked her off her feet. There was no vegetation to keep the sand of Otherwhere in place. The discharge tossed sharp, nasty grit into the air. She threw up a shield to protect her skin from being shredded. Granted, her nanites would rebuild the tissue within seconds, but having skin sanded off still hurt like a mother.

As the dust settled, she climbed to her feet and reached out with her senses. Surprisingly, the three humans were still alive despite their proximity to the lightning strike.

Sam considered the situation as she jogged toward the living people. She'd never encountered any kind of weather in Otherwhere other than the constant wind. It was a question for her counterpart deities, but first, she needed to get the humans out of here. They were way too close to the amphitheater.

Shit, had they entered the Conclave of Death? If they had, they were doomed. Even the deities of death couldn't stop the demise of a living entity stupid enough to walk into this particular amphitheater. As much as Sam wanted to kick Baron Samedi's ass for bringing her very mortal brother Max here, she'd screwed up in how she dealt with one of the Baron's disciples.

"What the hell, bitch?" one of the humans screamed. "I needed that thing to get home!"

Someone replied in a language that seem to be a weird combination of Latin, Old English, and—Chumash? But the feminine voice sounded just as pissed as the first speaker.

"Stop yelling!" a third person shouted to be heard over the other two. "We're going to need to work together in order to get out of this place."

Sam rounded the Conclave and spotted the three humans near the amphitheater's entrance. She slowed to a walk before she yelled, "Can anyone join this fight?"

The three women shut up and stared at her. Well, the chick with the red eyes and dressed all in black barely glanced at Sam before she fell to her knees, whimpered in pain, and pulled her hood over her face.

"Who are you?" the lady in the helmet and fancy motorcycle-style jacket and pants demanded.

"My name's Sam Ridgeway St. James." Sam wasn't fond of the length of her name, but it made her husband Duncan happy when she added his surname to the list. She examined the cowering woman in black. No, not cowering. More like someone desperately trying to shield herself from an environmental danger.

"Hi, Sam. I'm Shan Wong-Washington," the youngest woman replied. She was dressed in a t-shirt and knit shorts. A copper knife with a bent tip dangled from her shorts' waist tie, but the fae-forged blade concerned Sam more.

Shan crouched next to the woman in black and murmured in Mandarin Chinese.

The woman in black answered, but her words were moderately different in pronunciation than the current version of the language. She also spoke in a stilting pace, like someone who's still learning a foreign language.

"Anthea says you are too bright." Shan frowned. "She said me and—" The young woman looked up at Ms. Helmet Head.

"Seriously?" Ms. Helmet Head perched her gloved fists on her hips. "You don't recognize me?"

Sam cocked her head. "Look, Karen, we do not have time to play a game of 'Don't you know who I am.'" A yowl above and behind them split the air. She didn't have to turn around to know what was behind her. "The birdcats already have your scent, and if we don't get out of here now, we're all going to end up on their menu."

"We don't even know where here is," Ms. Helmet Head shot back.

"You're in Otherwhere," Sam said.

"Let me guess. It's next door to Neverland?" With that level of sarcasm, the woman in the odd brown and gray biker outfit would fit in with Sam's family and friends. But while Sam admired the woman's snark, it would get her killed quicker than she knew.

"Look, Ms. Helmet Head," Sam growled. "Shan introduced herself and her buddy. And if you want to stay here and get your soul eaten, that's your issue. I'm getting the other people who aren't giving me shit back to Los Angeles."

"Los Angeles?" The figure flipped up its visor to reveal an attractive Black woman, her face framed with short red dreads. "Aisha Franklin-Garcia, also known as the Ghost Owl."

"You think you're a superhero?" Sam wasn't sure why she was surprised. In fact, it was a wonder more supernaturals didn't run around in tights. Since the Great Revelation, it would be a way to get the Normal community to accept the supernatural races.

Aisha scowled at her. "I don't think. I *am* a superhero."

Nope, not dealing with this kind of craziness in the middle of Otherwhere. Sam turned to Shan. "What did Anthea say about you and Aisha?"

"That we glowed, but not as bright as you."

That made sense. Anthea was a witch. Since the other two women were demigoddesses, she could see the truth in their auras. However, every witch Sam had ever run into said her own aura was black because she was technically dead. So what made her blinding to this strange witch's sight?

"This is getting ridiculous." Sam shook her head. "We need to be able to talk to each other directly." She reached for Anthea, who scrabbled backward on her hands and feet and kept her eyes screwed shut. The robed woman shouted something in her incomprehensible mishmash language.

However, Sam moved faster. She grabbed Anthea's skull and implanted English in the woman's brain before the witch could raise her mental shields.

"—me go, you demon spawn—" She stopped shrieking abruptly, but not from Sam releasing her head. "How? How am I speaking a foreign language?" Anthea actually sounded curious though she kept her eyes closed.

"Because it's a lot easier for the rest of us to understand you than poor Shan translating your mangled Mandarin," Sam retorted.

"Man-dar-in?" Anthea spoke the word like she was testing it. "Shan spoke an odd version of Jing."

"Uh, maybe we can debate the language issue when we get to L.A., guys." Aisha stared up over Sam's head. "There's a lot more of your birdcat friends on top of the amphitheater, Sam."

She looked over her shoulder. Aisha was right. The multi-colored gleam of hundreds of birdcat eyes shone from the top of the basalt wall, and their feathery tails twitched in anticipation of a feast. There were more than Sam could fight by herself without losing one or more of the humans. They needed to get the hell out of Otherwhere. Now.

Sam bent and hoisted Anthea in her arms. "Aisha, please tell me you have superstrength and speed."

She nodded and slid her visor back into place before she picked up Shan.

"This is thoroughly embarrassing," Anthea muttered.

Sam ignored the witch. She turned and raced for the nearest crossroads.

CHAPTER 9

The last thing Anthea wanted was to die helplessly. She'd rather give her life with her sword in her hand and killing demons. Or these strange birdcats chasing them. It made her sick she was out of her league in the strange world she followed the demon to. But the woman who carried her glowed like the vision of Balance she had during the Battle of Tandor.

Yet, she called herself Sam Ridgeway St. James. She didn't claim she was one of the Twelve. The only one to make any sort of claim was Aisha, but she didn't say she was a deity. What in the Twelve was a superhero anyway?

The yowling of the birdcats fell further behind them. Sam ran with the steady rhythm of a long-distance messenger despite the sand, but Anthea couldn't hear the second set of footsteps that would indicate Aisha was keeping up with them while carrying Shan.

"Sam, did we lose the other two?"

"Nope. They're with us. Ms. Helmet Head left out that she could fly."

"She has a second form of a bird?"

Sam laughed. "No, she's not a were."

"A were?"

"A human who can shift into an animal form," Sam said. It was astounding. She wasn't even out of breath from talking while she ran.

"We call them Wildlings," Anthea said. "But if she doesn't have a second form with wings—"

"We can trade stories once I get you three to a safe place." The sound of Sam's steps went from the swish of sand to the rapid clicks of boots on cobblestones.

"Oh, my god," Shan said from above Anthea. "What is this place?"

"It almost looks like someone set off a nuke in downtown Los Angeles, and the buildings melted." Aisha's voice was muffled because of the strange helm she wore, but she sounded and felt as emotionally disturbed as Shan.

Worse, something kept pace with them from the nearby clattering of stones. Anthea didn't dare reach out with her psyche. Instead, she whispered, "Sam, we have more company than the birdcats."

"I know," she muttered. "We're almost to the crossroads."

"I can stop time around the beast, but I would need to borrow your eyes without you roasting my brain in my skull," Anthea said.

"You can what?"

"You heard me the first time," Anthea grumbled. Someone this powerful couldn't be this foolish.

"That's way beyond the skills of the witches I know." *How's this?*

It felt like a sasquatch holding perfectly still while a butterfly sat on their hand. Anthea wasn't sure she liked being the butterfly in this particular scenario. Sam could kill her with a thought, but all that terrible power was kept in check.

Good, Anthea replied. The shining woman's senses were greater than Anthea's measly human ones, even better than her odd sight. There were at least five beasts pacing them from the sounds of them running on the gravel scattered across the cracked and broken pavers. The intense colors in Sam's vision put Luc's normal sight to shame. And the smells. Embarrassment at her own body odor claimed Anthea. She'd just spent the morning in the Naha public baths to scrub away her stench after two months at sea.

You don't smell that bad. Sam's laughter tinkled like diamonds falling into a pile. *And I do appreciate you bathed this morning.*

Sam glanced to her right. Through her, Anthea spotted the closest beast. It was covered in black fur, but that was the only thing that seemed natural. The beast was taller than a horse and wider than a Plains bison. Its limbs were distorted as if its joints had been reversed, and it had so many sharp teeth it couldn't close its mouth properly.

Anthea added a touch of her psyche to Sam's vision and studied the lines of reality around them. The lines were thicker and slower than what she was used to dealing with, but the principles remained the same. She grabbed the threads of time winding around this place and the beast and jerked. The beast stumbled at her interruption of its stride. It crashed to the ground and knocked over a pillar of black stone upon itself.

Nice shot, Sam said silently.

More stone monoliths blocked Sam's view of the fallen beast in this strange twilight. But a moment later, a shrill scream of pain rent the air. The scream abruptly cut off, and the sounds of teeth tearing flesh replaced it.

"Its fellows are eating it?" Anthea asked.

"Only two of them," Sam answered. "Aisha, land right before the next crossroads. We'll be cutting this damn close."

"You're leaving us open for attack," Aisha protested.

"Don't have time to argue with you about it," Sam snapped. "Anthea, the two on our left—"

"If you can box them in the street, I can freeze them."

Sam slid to a halt before the open space and set Anthea on her feet though she kept the mental link between them.

Anthea swallowed the urge to draw her sword. The two remaining beasts approached from the broken roadway on their left. She started to step forward, but Sam grabbed her arm and yanked her back.

"Don't step into the crossroad until I say so. I don't want to lose you."

Aisha landed on the other side of Sam, but she kept Shan in her arms.

The shards of broken pavers would slice the swordwoman's canvas slippers and then her feet into shreds.

Sam crossed to the closest stone that had to be five stories tall. Through Sam's eyes, Anthea could see the tiny fractures of the basalt. Sam performed a perfect backspin kick, something Lady Shi Hua had been trying to teach Anthea for months. A slice of rock parted from the monolith and crashed onto the cross street.

The beasts skidded to a halt. They could probably leap the debris if they could get a good running start. The pair must have realized the same thing. They whirled around and headed back the way they came.

"Can I borrow one of your throwing knives?" Sam asked politely, but it was more of a command than a request.

Anthea slipped one from her robes and handed it hilt first to Sam, though a shiver ran through her at the image of her handing a weapon to herself.

Sam twisted and threw the steel blade at one of the monoliths behind the beasts. Right into a fissure Anthea was sure no one else but Sam could see. Cracks and snaps echoed along the decrepit street until a huge chunk split from the main part of the monolith and crashed across the pavers. The wreckage formed a near perfect square that would only trap the beasts for a few moments.

Anthea made the proper gestures and murmured the time freeze incantation. For once, she wasn't trying to twist an old spell into a new purpose. And it worked, but for Balance knew how long in this strange environment.

"Everyone grab hands," Sam ordered as she took Anthea's. The woman's presence left Anthea's mind when Aisha grasped Sam's other hand. "Take one step forward—now!"

A wave of dizziness swept over Anthea, similar to the one she experienced when she passed through the demon's portal in Naha. Sound roared through her and rattled her very bones. She turned her head away from

Sam and dared to open her eyes. The colors and images were as chaotic as the noise assaulting her ears. She closed her eyes again.

HONK!

Anthea jumped at the blast of sound.

"And a yippee-ki-yay, mother—" The rest of Sam's words were lost in another blast. She dragged Anthea several steps until she tripped over what felt like a rock. However, Sam didn't let her fall.

"Where are we?" Shan asked.

"Hill Street in downtown," Sam answered. "Hang on. One more 'port."

A third wave of vertigo made Anthea want to purge her stomach. However, the cacophony assaulting her ears abruptly disappeared.

"Sorry, but we can only exit through a crossroad in Otherwhere that matches an existing crossroad in this reality. From downtown Los Angeles, I can teleport almost anywhere else in this universe."

"Whose house is this?" Aisha asked.

"My house," a new female voice said. "What the hell, Sam? Your house is next door. You are such a schmuck."

"Cara Lannigan is on duty," Sam bit back. "And I didn't want her shooting my guests."

The sharp edge of Conflict magic touched Anthea's psyche. "I am Chief Justice Anthea of Orrin from the Queendom of Issura. We apologize for the intrusion, Sister. My companions and I were accidentally pulled into Otherwhere by demons. Sam was kind enough to rescue us before the other denizens could kill and eat us."

"Well, it's nice to see someone has manners. I'm Doctor Bebe Zachary." Feet rustled on carpet, and a brush of air stirred as the woman stepped closer. "Is there something wrong with your eyes? Why are they closed?"

"I find I have difficulty looking at Sam. She's blindingly bright white to me."

"Anthea says she can see Shan and Aisha's demigoddess auras, but I don't get why my aura is white to her," Sam added.

"Her eyes are red," Shan offered. "Could that effect her sight? Because Sam looks normal to me. Except how did you change your clothes?"

Sam sighed. "Long story."

"Tell it over lunch," Bebe said. "Ptolemy's making tacos. Let's see what I can do to help Anthea in the meantime. If nothing else, maybe some polarized sunglasses would work."

Anthea held out her left hand. It had been seventeen years since she was totally blind, but the old habits were so ingrained they irritated her.

Bebe carefully folded Anthea's hand around her elbow. She called out directions and paces as they strode out of the area where Sam had brought Anthea and the others and down a hallway from the echo of their footsteps on wood. Almost as if Bebe had graduated from the Warden Academy.

"Balance, I hate this," Anthea muttered under her breath.

"Hate what?" Bebe asked.

"Being led around like the queen's prized dogs."

Bebe laughed. "You're not fuzzy enough to be anyone's corgi."

"What is a corgi?"

"The breed of the queen of England's pet dogs," Bebe added.

Anthea smiled. "I do not know this queen of England or her preferred breeds, but Queen Teodora's original pair of xoloitzcuintli were a gift from the queen of Cant, and I guarantee that breed is not fuzzy as they are quite hairless."

"My apologies for misunderstanding, Chief Justice," Bebe murmured as she led Anthea into another room.

Anthea peeked, secure she was far enough away from Sam. The blinding white brilliance was gone, and she sighed in relief. "That's better."

Bebe paused in walking and looked up at Anthea. It was only the second time in her life someone watched her with curiosity, not fear.

She examined Bebe in turn. The other woman was roughly two hand-spans shorter than Anthea, and her blue hair was wildly curly, but not in the same way as those from the Cradle. Her thick cotton leggings ended above her knees, and her tunic had no sleeves and buttoned down the front. Instead of leather, her shoes were made of canvas like Shan's footwear, and they had an odd material for the soles.

"Have a seat," Bebe waved at one of the chairs in the room. "Were you born with red eyes?" She crossed to a cabinet and shuffled through a drawer.

"Actually, I was born blind. According to the healers, my eyes had formed correctly, but the nerves were damaged." Anthea looked around the room. It resembled a healer's examination room. Some items were constructed of steel and other metals, but most of the items were made of substances she couldn't identify.

"May I ask how you gained your physical sight?" Bebe laid instruments on an elevated tray with wheels.

Anthea chuckled. "I thought if I could give myself sight, I could escape Temple service. However, I had no true reference, and my spell warped my eyes so I can see after a fashion, but it's not like normal human vision."

"So what does my aura look like to you?" Bebe rolled the tray closer to Anthea.

"Your aura?"

"Yes." Bebe pushed a stool, also with wheels on its feet, closer to Anthea and sat. "Every witch has an aura about their body. The primary color depends on the element of magic they wield."

"Really?" The new information puzzled Anthea. "No one has ever mentioned auras to me. What do these auras look like to you?"

"They resemble light energy emanating from a person," Bebe explained. "Sam said you could see the other two women's auras."

"You mean the white light surrounding Aisha and Shan?"

Bebe chuckled. "Their auras aren't white to me, but yes."

"Curious." Anthea considered the logic of the situation. "What color is mine to you?"

"Yours is a pale purple." Bebe smiled. "Mine is a golden yellow."

Anthea cocked her head. "So these auras are not the same color as the Temple you serve?"

"That's the second time you've mentioned Temples." Bebe frowned. "Are you a priestess?"

"All justices are priestesses of the Temple of Balance, and we are all blind except me."

"I have a ton of questions, but let me check your eyes first." Bebe held up a metal cylinder with a cone made of one of the odd materials attached to the top. "There's a light on this so I can see into your eye. Normally, it doesn't affect the patient, but if it hurts you, let me know, and I'll stop."

Anthea leaned away from the other woman. "Why are you doing this? How can you be a healer?"

"I'm not a healer." The corners of Bebe's mouth twitched. "I'm a doctor."

Anthea shook her head. "When Sam gifted me with your language, I fear she left out a few things. What is a doctor?"

"Someone who has been trained to help people who are sick or injured, but they don't have any healing magick." Bebe waved her free hand. "Like a physician."

"Oh, I understand now." Anthea nodded. "You are a Conflict priestess trained by the Healers Guild to care for injured in battle."

Bebe's right eyebrow rose. "Not every person with magickal talent is a clergyperson here."

"Not everyone with talent is a clergyperson in Issura either, but someone as powerful as yourself would be claimed by the Temples."

"We are really getting off track here." Bebe raised her cylinder to her right eye. The cone glowed a faint yellow. "Does the light bother you?"

"No." Anthea didn't want to admit she couldn't see the light. While she wanted to trust Sam and her friend, she wasn't sure exactly what, much less where, she had stumbled into. The only reassuring thing about the people she met in this Otherwhere is that demons didn't glow. That didn't mean they couldn't wear a human skin like Bebe's.

"All right." Bebe lowered the cylinder after examining both of Anthea's eyes through the device and rolled her stool back a yard. "What's the smallest line you can read on that chart?" She pointed at a paper affixed to the opposite wall.

"I cannot read it."

"Oh, crap. I'm sorry" Bebe's chagrin flowed over Anthea's outer shields. "Sam gave you spoken English, but not our alphabet or numbers."

Anthea winced. "Actually, that's not the problem. I have a difficult time discerning dried ink from paper or parchment."

"What color was the light I used on you?" Bebe asked.

Anthea's shoulders sagged. "I could not see the light itself, but the cone at the top glowed yellow."

Bebe touched the top of her device. It glowed yellow again for a moment, and a thoughtful expression crossed her face. "What color are my hair and skin to you?"

"Blue and yellow." Anthea frowned because she couldn't follow the other woman's path of thought. "Why?"

"May I include you in a telepathic conversation with Sam?"

"Telepathic?"

"It's a method of communication without using our voices."

You mean silent speech? Anthea said.

Bebe laughed. *You are a fascinating person, Chief Justice.*

"Please call me Anthea." She smiled at the physician. "I'm not a chief justice here in England."

"Los Angeles isn't in England," Bebe said. "We're in the United States of America. In fact, we rebelled and broke away from England about two hundred and fifty years ago."

That piece of news was unnerving. The Temples did their best to keep the civilian authorities and the populace from doing idiotic things. It went to show what happened when a world wasn't unified, human nature being what it was.

As you said, please speak with Sam, and then we can exchange information about our cultures over your tacos, Anthea said.

"Sam, I think I've figured out the issue with Anthea's sight," Bebe said both out loud and silently.

And? Sam's mental voice sounded impatient.

"She has infrared vision. Can you tone down your emissions on that end of the spectrum?"

Anthea frowned. Bebe's terms were strange. Apparently, Sam's gift of their language only worked when there was a corresponding word in one of the languages Anthea already knew.

After several long moments, Sam added, *Okay, it should be safe for you guys to come out now. Aisha says she's not picking up any extreme infrared signals from me.*

"Ready?" Bebe stood.

Anthea rose to her feet. "I believe so."

"I can't wait to introduce you to tacos!"

Anthea sent a little prayer to the Twelve that these tacos were edible. But after nearly two months aboard the *Mars Tranquilus*, anything that wasn't fish or dried should be delicious.

CHAPTER 10

Shan suddenly realized she was a guest in someone's home. Someone's very nice home like the mansion on Long Island where she and Jamal attended a Halloween party when they were in college. And she still wore her pajamas. Aisha and Anthea may be wearing weird clothes, but they had everything covered. Sam had somehow transformed her coat, slacks, and boots into a t-shirt, jeans, and sneakers. Shan, on the other hand, was very conscious she wasn't wearing panties or a bra beneath her sleepwear.

"Uh, I hate to be ungrateful, but could I borrow something to wear?" she said.

"Food first," Sam said. "You can't tell me you aren't starving after fighting for your life in Otherwhere. Then we'll get you some clothes."

"But—"

"Honey, your bits are covered," Sam assured her.

Aisha unlatched her helmet from her jacket and pulled it off. "I know I could use some tacos. It was close to lunchtime when I got called to Allen George Memorial Park." She leaned closer to Shan. "And you're not the only one wearing just shorts and a t-shirt."

"I'll bet you have a bra on," Shan said sourly. "I was woken out of a dead sleep when that creature broke into my mother-in-law's store."

Sam beckoned Shan and Aisha to follow her. "Why on earth were you sleeping in your mother-in-law's store?"

"My husband and I rent the second story loft from her and her cousin." Shan paced after Sam and grimaced as she tracked sand through Bebe's immaculate home. She would volunteer to run the vacuum after she ate and took a shower. "And they're giving us a huge discount considering the rents in Greenwich Village in return for babysitting—oh, shit! I left the girls alone!"

Sam stopped in midstride as they entered the foyer. "You have kids?"

"No, it's Jamal's baby sister Tanja and their cousin's daughter Livvy." Shan couldn't breathe with the panic coursing through her veins. "They're both only nine."

"Take a deep breath, Shan." Aisha wrapped an arm around her shoulders. "If you disappeared last night, they would've called their parents, wouldn't they?"

Shan nodded. "I told them to lock themselves in the bathroom and call 9-1-1. And Cu Chulainn was with them."

"Cu Chulainn?" Aisha asked.

"He was an Irish folk hero, the son of—" Sam glared at Shan. No, not at her. At Lexi. "That's why I'm sensing fae magick. That's what caused the first explosion. You and Anthea both cast spells—"

"I didn't cast any spell," Shan protested. "The creature that pulled me into your Otherwhere exploded when we both stabbed it."

Sam rolled her eyes. "I haven't had enough caffeine yet today to deal with fae shit." She turned and continued stalking across the marble floor of the foyer.

Shan looked up at Aisha. "What does she have against the Tuatha?"

"I'm not one hundred percent certain." The taller woman frowned. "But if she is what I think she might be, it's probably a pantheon rivalry."

"Do you really think so?" The same shiver ran through Shan that had when Grandmother Wong admitted she was Kwan Yin.

"My mother-in-law is Xquic, a Mayan deity." Aisha sighed. "She bestowed my powers on me while I was pregnant so I could protect her grandchildren. It would explain why poor Anthea said we glowed, but she couldn't look at Sam." She grinned at Shan. "But I'm not turning down food, and I really hope they have some diet cola. Sam's not the only one who hasn't had enough caffeine today."

"Well, as long as it's just us women," Shan muttered.

She followed the other two women through a swinging door and stopped in total shock. The man standing at the huge range and stirring ground beef in a skillet was the spitting image of her cousin Jake. Her older cousin who'd died in a freak accident years ago.

"What's wrong?" Aisha asked.

"Are we dead?" Shan whispered.

"No," Sam said emphatically. "I couldn't bring you to Bebe's house if you were."

The man looked up and smirked. "Speaking of which, why can't you take your strays to your own home, Samantha?"

Shan swallowed hard. Jake's doppelganger didn't have his southern California accent. This guy sounded vaguely European with something else mixed in.

"Ladies, this is Bebe's brother-in-law Ptolemy Philadelphus Antonius," Sam said.

"And I call bullshit." Aisha smiled sweetly. "He died two thousand years ago."

The man Sam and Bebe called Ptolemy laid down his wooden spoon in a ceramic spoon holder. "Sam speaks truly. I am Ptolemy Philadelphus. I happen to live in the body of a man named Jake Wong."

It was too much in the last few hours. Shan's vision went black, and once again, she was falling into an abyss.

Something cold, rough, and wet stroked Shan's face. "Cu Chulainn, stop. Did the Tanja give you a popsicle again?" She swiped at the offending tongue.

And met skin.

She checked again. Nope, not enough fur to be the Irish wolfhound.

She opened her eyes. She lay on the kitchen floor. Sam, Aisha, and the guy in her cousin's body crouched around her with concerned expressions.

Shan groaned and closed her eyes again. "Damn, I really hoped I had a nightmare."

"Honey, what happened?" Aisha stroked her forehead with the damp washcloth. "You stared at Ptolemy like you'd seen a ghost."

Shan swallowed hard. "M-my cousin Jake died in an accident ten years ago. H-he was a stuntman and so cool. He used to take me riding on his Harley despite my dad's freakouts over motorcycles."

"Shit," Sam muttered. "I'm so sorry, Shan. It didn't even register with me when you said your surname was Wong."

"Where do you live, child?" It was definitely Jake's voice, but again, he had an odd accent she couldn't quite place. And he never looked down at her because of their age difference.

"Greenwich Village." A tear rolled down Shan's temple, and she sniffed to keep more from escaping.

"In New York City?" he asked.

She nodded.

"Our Jake has a second cousin Chen who is a thoracic surgeon in New York," he mused. "His daughter Shan is an engineer."

Shan's eyes popped open. "In what world does my cousin come back from the dead? Eddie and Audra had to have a closed casket because Jake's skull was caved in!"

At the weird looks Ptolemy and Sam exchanged, the dam burst and Shan couldn't stop the sobs wracking her chest.

"It's okay." Aisha sat next to Shan and held her. "It's okay. We'll figure this all out."

"And?" Sam snapped.

"What the hell is wrong with you?" Aisha shot back.

Sam waved impatiently, and her eyes were focused on something Shan couldn't see.

"She and Bebe are discussing something via telepathy," Ptolemy said.

"Telepathy?" Shan asked.

He grinned. It wasn't quite like the devil-may-care smile of her cousin Jake, but it was close enough it sent a pang of grief through her. "Yes. I used to be able to do it, but now that I'm human again—" He shrugged.

"Ghosts are telepathic?" she asked.

"No, but vampires are."

"Vampires?"

"Oh, shit," Sam muttered. "How am I supposed to test how much infra-red radiation I'm giving off?"

"Whoa." Aisha helped Shan into a sitting position. "How did we go from tacos, ghosts, and telepathy to the low end of the EM spectrum?"

"Don't forget the vampires," Shan added dryly.

"Apparently, Anthea sees infrared," Sam said. "That's why I'm too bright for her to look at. I think I know how to tone down my emissions on the lower band, but I have no way of testing it."

"If we were in my lab, I could, but—" Shan shrugged helplessly.

"If my suit's computer wasn't fried, I could." Aisha said.

"Heads-up display on your visor?" Shan asked.

Aisha nodded and handed Shan her helmet. "You think you can fix it?"

"It would take more than I have here to fix the entire suit, but if I can get the visor display to work . . ." Shan examined interior of the helmet. The amount of talent put into it was freakin' amazing. She unplugged the pow-er line and grinned to herself. The designer was freakin' brilliant. "Ptolemy, you wouldn't happen to have a Maxiphone charger, would you?"

CHAPTER 11

Aisha stripped off her supersuit in the kitchen since their hosts insisted on eating before anything else. It was a bit of relief to shed the armored outfit. Without the computer, she had no environmental systems, and she was roasting in the damn thing.

While Aisha ate, she watched Shan examine her helmet. The younger woman had chowed down three tacos before she was again distracted by the tech in Aisha's Ghost Owl suit. Bebe had checked Shan's blood sugar level and determined that had contributed to her fainting. Something a glass of orange juice had rectified.

Aisha worried about the radiation her suit's computer registered when the monster dragged her through its portal. While she was fairly certain she hadn't experienced any ill effects, she wondered what the radiation bursts may have done to Shan and Anthea. But Bebe seemed to have similar abilities to Serena, the physician's assistant who lived on Aisha's block and was also a super. The doctor assured Sam that their three guests were healthy.

Apparently, Anthea was familiar with the concept of breakfast tacos. She exhibited sheer delight Bebe had hot sauce as well though she said it had a slightly different taste than what she referred to as Cantan sauce, and she politely requested Ptolemy's taco meat recipe. Bebe had to translate a couple of spices into their witch names, but Anthea assured Ptolemy her cook had all the ingredients and looked forward to toasting tortillas into hard taco shells.

"This is a custom motherboard." Shan looked at Aisha. "Did you make this?"

Aisha shook her head. "My predecessor as the Ghost Owl created the suit. He didn't have any actual powers so he built the suit to compensate when he battled supervillains."

"Let me guess," Sam said around a mouthful of taco. "He was your dad, and you became the Ghost Owl to avenge his death."

"Um, not exactly." Aisha sipped her diet soda to keep from making a snarky comment about Sam reading too many comic books. With the monster who dragged her into this mess dead, she needed these people's help if she wanted to see Rey and Mitch ever again.

"Ignore her," Ptolemy said. "Her paparazzi tendencies show at the worst possible times."

"You're a goddess, and you work for a tabloid?" Aisha stared at the blonde. She probably shouldn't have blurted the truth in front of Anthea. The red-eyed witch seemed pretty religious.

Sam shook her head. "I worked for the *National Scoop* when I was alive." She swallowed her bite of taco. "After I died, I became an agent for a trio that does a retro act in Las Vegas."

Aisha frowned. "I've never heard of the *National Scoop*."

"It could be we each come from an alternate timeline," Shan suggested.

"You mean like the Many-Worlds theory?" Aisha asked.

Shan nodded. "It would explain why my Jake is dead and Sam's is still here."

"As far as Jake's family is concerned, he's still alive," Ptolemy said. "There was never a funeral for our Shan to attend."

Aisha popped the last bite of taco into her mouth. Shan's idea was the only thing that made sense. Or else Rey had made Aisha watch one too many science fiction movies after they put Mitch to bed.

"May I ask a question of Sam first before we continue discussing your theory?" Anthea said.

"Sure." Sam took another bite of taco.

"Which one of the Twelve are you?"

Sam chewed slowly. "No offense, but I have no idea what you're talking about."

"Aisha referred to you as a goddess." Anthea gestured at Aisha, and she wanted to hide under the table. "It would explain why I could not initially look directly at you."

"Um, I think your religion may be different than the ones the rest of us know," Aisha said. "I don't mean to be rude or disrespectful, but could you explain it a little more?"

"More than one religion?" Again, Anthea got a thoughtful expression as she worked through to her next question. "Your worlds have not been unified by Balance?"

"What is Balance?" Aisha asked.

"She is the first of the Twelve." Anthea looked as confused as Aisha felt.

"So she's like the mother of all," Shan offered.

Anthea smiled. "Mother is her second form as Death is her third."

"So you know a version of the Triple Goddess." Bebe smiled.

"In a sense." Anthea nodded before she turned back to Sam.

"Oh, shit," the blonde murmured and buried her face in her hands.

"You need to answer her question," Aisha prodded.

Sam lifted her head and glared at her. "It's not that simple."

Aisha turned to Anthea. "In my world, and I'm sure in this world, too, there's multiple versions of the deities. For example, my mother-in-law is one of the Mayan death goddesses." She nudged Shan with her elbow.

The younger woman looked up with wide brown eyes. "Um, I'm not supposed to be talking about this."

"Hey, if you're glowing like I am to Anthea, then you've got god blood in your background," Aisha prodded.

"Oh, for the love of—one of Shan's ancestors is the mother goddess of China," Sam snapped. "But I want to know how you ended up with that sword." She jabbed a finger at Shan's sword standing in the corner behind her.

The sword squealed back at Sam.

"Lexi is technically my husband's." Shan narrowed her eyes. "It's been passed down through his family. Why do you hate the Tuatha so much?"

Sam's mouth opened, and she abruptly closed it so hard her teeth clicked. Ptolemy and Bebe's snickers filled out the rest of the story.

"What did you do to piss off the fairies, Sam?" Aisha said.

Bebe, Ptolemy, and Sam all gasped aloud.

Ptolemy cleared his throat. "That term is actually a racial slur for the fae here. Please don't use it again. It took my wife a long time and a tremendous amount of political capital to broker the peace treaty between the Vampire Nation and the Sidhe Courts."

"I'm sorry," Aisha said sincerely. She had all too much experience in her life with bigots. "Thank you for correcting me. I won't use it again."

"Technically, Sam didn't start the feud," Bebe said. "It existed for thousands of years between the fae and the vampires. Sam was the guinea pig in experiments to cure the vampires of their reactions to sunlight, silver, and garlic while keeping their lack of aging, longevity—"

"And their ability to turn into bats?" Aisha added.

Sam snorted. "Throw out any pop culture beliefs about vampires. They don't need an invitation to enter your home, religious icons don't affect them, and their condition is caused by a virus related to Ebola. If you're infected and you don't receive treatment before you go into a coma, there's a ninety percent chance of you dying."

She inhaled deeply before she turned to Anthea. "To answer your question, I am a goddess of death in this universe. More specifically, I am the vampires' goddess of death. I was on my way back here after checking on the afterlife I'm responsible for when I ran across you three." She smiled wryly. "If you only have one Death, what are they like?"

Anthea sat back in her chair and gripped the cup of brewed tea she had requested. "According to our Books, she collects us when our spirit leaves our body and delivers us to Light."

"This Light is another goddess?" Aisha asked.

"God," Anthea corrected. She proceeded to explain how Balance had come to the World nearly two thousand years ago. The Twelve were defined by their roles and responsibilities, not by the various tribal and village names humans bestowed on them. Balance called all the World's religious leaders together and essentially told them to cut the bullshit because a malevolent species would invade soon. If the humans didn't start working together, the invaders, whom the humans referred to as demons, would literally devour their world.

"We had a thousand years to prepare, and we've been fighting the demons for nearly a thousand more years." Anthea lifted her cup and realized it was empty.

Bebe stood and held out her hand for the mug. "I'll make you some more."

"Thank you," Anthea murmured.

Aisha looked at Shan. "Were there more demons in your mother-in-law's shop besides the one that dragged you to Otherwhere?"

Shan shook her head. "Just the one." She scowled. "It seemed terribly interested in a strange grimoire a woman brought in right before we closed.

Phylicia had already left for the evening, and the woman offered to leave it with me in order for my mother-in-law to appraise it."

An alarmed expression spread over Anthea's face. "Did you touch it?"

"Yes." Shan frowned. "It had some kind of weird leather, and I didn't recognize the language it was written in—"

"Do you hear voices in your head?" Anthea persisted.

"What? No!" Shan protested.

"If we—" Anthea closed her eyes for a few seconds, trying to compose herself. "When we get home, you need to destroy that grimoire. It is made from the demons' dead and the grimoires corrupt those of us with talent. If your mother-in-law is talented, she is in terrible danger."

"You mean people like you and Bebe who can perform magic?" Aisha asked.

Anthea nodded, a grave expression on her face.

Shan turned sheet white. "Tanja and Livvy are talented, too, and they're alone at the loft."

"Hang in there, Shan." Aisha squeezed the younger woman's shoulder. "We'll figure out a way for all of us to get home. But while we're here, Anthea can teach us how to deal with these menaces so we're prepared when we do get back."

She hoped she hadn't just lied her ass off to Shan. It would kill her if Rey and Mitch met the same fate as the boy in the park.

And that thought was as terrifying as never seeing her husband and son again.

CHAPTER 12

Sam pulled her phone out of her jeans pocket and tapped out a text to Tiffany. Her sister-in-law's doctorate in physics may just pay off in this situation.

"Who are you contacting?" Bebe said.

Ptolemy smirked as he leaned over Sam's arm. "My wife."

"The research she's doing on quantum vibrations may help me get these ladies back to where they belong." Sam set her phone aside before she grabbed two more tacos from the serving platter.

"You actually understood her?" Ptolemy mocked.

Sam shrugged. "Some of it. More than you did."

"I beg your pardon?"

Her phone buzzed. Ignoring the offended Egyptian prince, she picked up the device to check the incoming text.

"Tiffany says she may be able to run some tests on us for comparison, but it'll have to be after her doctorate students finish with their experiment late this afternoon." Sam sighed and laid down her phone on the table again. "She'll text me once the lab is clear."

She eyed Shan whose fascination with Aisha's equipment was the only reason the younger woman was still awake. "It's going to be a few hours before I can teleport you ladies to Cal Tech. Why don't you get showers and take naps while you can?"

"Maybe get some fresh clothes, too?" Aisha asked hopefully.

"Since you and Anthea are close to my size, I'll go next door and raid my closet." Sam pushed to her feet.

"I know it's a lot to ask, but could I please get some underwear?" Shan's pleading expression made Sam feel a bit sorry for the younger woman.

It reminded Sam too much of her own embarrassment when she'd been kidnapped. The stupid mad scientists had cut off Sam's clothes before they started their experiment on her. When she had woken, she desperately searched for something to wear after she died because she didn't want to escape clad in only a hospital gown with her naked ass hanging out the back.

In comparison, Shan wasn't in that bad of shape.

"Get your shower and a nap, Shan." Sam smiled. "I promise I'll have brand-new, clean undies and sports bras for all three of you when you wake up."

"I'm not working on the jetlag Shan and Anthea are," Aisha said. "Would you mind if I tag along on the shopping trip?" She reached into a pocket on the inside of her boot and held up a credit card and cash. "At least, I can buy the coffee."

After checking with her head of security Connie Torres to confirm Cara Lannigan had left for the day, Sam teleported Aisha and herself next door to the kitchen in her own house.

"Whoa!" Aisha grabbed the granite counter to steady herself. "We couldn't just walk across the yard and jump the fence?"

"Not without getting a couple of clips emptied in your ass by the guards," Connie said as she walked into the kitchen. She eyed the superhero with more than a bit of suspicion. "What the hell were you thinking, Sam? This chica is your Mayan sister's." She waved a hand in Aisha's directions. "Are you trying to start problems with another pantheon? Is life too peaceful for you?"

"Quit yer bitchin'," Sam snapped. "Aisha doesn't belong to our version of reality. She's from an alternate Earth. How are we doing in the spare clothes closet?"

"We have nothing remotely in your size as far as street clothes right now." Connie crossed her arms, and her hazel eyes started to glow neon yellow. "Not to mention, we're totally out of sports bras and panties in your size."

Her mood abruptly gentled and the glow of her eyes faded when she faced Aisha. "I've got everything set up for you in one of the guest rooms. You're lucky you're better endowed than the boss, and I still had some larger sizes." She grabbed her own C-cups to emphasize her point.

"Hey!" Sam protested.

Connie continued talking to their guest like Sam hadn't said a thing. "I've got some things packed for you and Shan for the next couple of days. I laid out clothes for you on your bed for when you're done in the bathroom."

"How did you know—" Aisha started.

Connie tapped her temple. "Telepathy. Sam told me your names and your sizes. Don't worry. We won't read your mind without permission. Sam learned to size up other women from the snobby Beverly Hills bitch she calls Mom."

A wry smile crossed Aisha's features, but she didn't comment on the description of Mom. Sam sighed. Besides, Connie was totally right about Mom's attitude and how she learned sizing while growing up.

"Besides, what I understand from the people in my universe with that particular gift, it's a lot harder to keep other people's thoughts out than to read them," Aisha said.

"Truth." Connie held up her palm, and Aisha high-fived her. "What's worse is when the ability kicks in and you're accidentally transmitting every stupid thing that crosses your mind to everyone around you."

"Amen." Sam held up her hand, but the other two women ignored her.

"I'll show you your room." Connie beckoned for Aisha to follow her.

"Wait," Sam blurted. "I need some clothes for Anthea, and she's about my size."

Connie glared at Sam. "Like I told you at the beginning of the year, I will replace your sizes when I inventory the stock room at the beginning of every month. If you use up those items before the end of the month, it's on you to replace them."

"I really miss when you were a vampire, and I could kick your ass to the sun," Sam growled.

Connie looked at the ceiling. "Hey, Phil! Sam's throwing a temper tantrum again!"

A soft pop of displaced air came from behind Sam. Aisha jumped back. Connie smirked. Wearily, Sam turned around and faced one of her closest friends.

"I apologize for Connie doing that, Phil," Sam said as contritely as she could manage considering her temper was about to explode after the morning she'd had. "But I'm glad you're here. I have a couple of questions about a new type of demon I encountered."

The former Amazon turned goddess smiled and shook her head. The chestnut curls that escaped her messy bun bounced with the motion. "Only you would deliberately seek out new enemies to vanquish."

"I didn't seek them out." Sam waved in her guest's direction. "Phillippa Mann, this is Aisha Franklin-Garcia. Aisha, this is Phil. She's family, but I would need a billboard and a 12-point font to explain all of the connections."

Sam turned back to Phil. "Aisha and two other women, a witch and another demigoddess, were dragged into Otherwhere by a type of demon I didn't recognize."

Phil frowned. "But not a dino demon?"

"Dino demons are still carbon-based. Even their acidic blood is related to the hydrochloric acid in our stomachs," Sam said. "The other two ladies, Anthea and Shan, killed two of the weird demons, and their guts that were splattered all over the sand of Otherwhere were silicon-based."

"Silicon-based?" Phil's expression turned to disbelief. "That's not possible."

"Bebe took some samples from the ladies' clothing. She needs to run the tests to confirm it." Sam shrugged. "But I swear it looked, felt, and smelled like the gel plastic surgeons used to use in boob implants."

"I wish they kept one of them alive so we could force it to take us home," Aisha grumbled.

"No offense, but I doubt if you three could have controlled one." Sam turned and marched over to the refrigerator. She retrieved a bottle of diet soda and held it up. "Want one, Aisha?"

"Yes, please."

Sam tossed it to her, and the Black woman neatly caught the bottle. "Go take your shower. I'll fill in Phil and Connie on events so far. You can add anything else once you get back downstairs." She pulled out another bottle for herself.

"Follow me." Connie beckoned once again and Aisha trailed after her.

Once they left the kitchen, Sam waited until the shower in the farthest guestroom spurted to life. "Would your dad have some ideas?" She set her cola bottle on the breakfast bar and turned to grab the tea kettle from the stove to heat water for Phil.

"I don't know." Phil retrieved a mug and the loose leaf tea from their cupboards. Sam suppressed a smile and pulled a brewing egg out of the utensil drawer. No modern teabags for her five-hundred-year-old husband Duncan or any of the folks older than him like Phil.

Phil concentrated while she scooped the loose tea into the bottom half of the egg. "But it's not going to hurt if we do." She screwed on the other half of the steeping egg and set the utensil in her mug.

Sam didn't like the idea of owing Ares of Olympus yet another favor. However, she needed to get her Lost Girls home without opening up her universe to invasion by these silicon bastards. Her Earth couldn't afford a thousand-year war after what she did to Puget Sound by blocking a dinosaur god from entering her universe.

CHAPTER 13

Anthea tossed and turned on the bed in the room Bebe had assigned her. Despite her exhaustion, she couldn't sleep. It had nothing to do with the incredibly luxurious personal quarters or the very soft bed covers and mattress. Or even Bebe's husband's odd sleepwear, which was very similar to the clothing Shan wore when they first met.

No, her lack of rest was due to her worries. What had happened to Luc after she fell through the demon portal? Queen Teodora had tasked them with protecting Crown Prince, soon to be emperor, Bao Quan Po and his bride Lady Shi Hua during their voyage back to Jing.

Captain Titus had docked the *Mars Tranquilus* in the port of Naha in the island kingdom of Ryukyu for repairs after two battles with skinwalkers, humans who practiced demon magic, while the Issuran ship crossed the Peaceful Sea. Of course, the king of Ryukyu had invited the future Jing emperor to dine at his palace. And when the future emperor and his escort entered Naha's central city square, they were ambushed by demons at the palace gates.

Quan's wife and his bodyguard tried to get him through the gates of the Crimson Palace, but the massive steel doors had slammed shut before the Jing party could reach them. Anthea had no idea if Quan, Shi Hua, or any of the combined Jing and Issuran escort had survived the battle. And she tried very hard not to envision the fate of her beloved Luc.

What in the Twelve had she been thinking? Bitterness filled her. She'd been so focused on killing the demon she chased that she paid no attention to her surroundings. Despite the danger, Thief made sure she ended up in Sam's Otherwhere instead of the demons' home dimension. Furthermore, she was lucky Sam found her and the other two women trapped in that terrible place. But there was no guarantee Sam could get them home. Aisha was right. She should have kept one demon alive in order to return all of them to their homes.

Anthea rolled onto her back and stared at the painted plaster ceiling, so different than the marble of her own quarters at the Orrin Temple of Balance. Now, she found herself depending on Sam as a representative of Death to get her home. Maybe that's what truly disturbed her. Nearly everyone she personally knew accused her of courting Death. Had she actually received what she thought she desired most? Just when she'd found some peace in her life?

There was a soft knock on her bedroom door.

Anthea reached out with her psyche. Shan stood in the hallway. Their hostess had no objection to any of her guests retaining their weapons, but Anthea didn't sense any ill intent from the woman who spoke an odd version of Jing.

Enter, Anthea said silently and sat upright.

Shan slipped inside and closed the door behind her. "I'm sorry if I'm intruding, but I couldn't sleep." Her anxiety hissed and fizzed like the head on a good ale.

"You're worried about your family," Anthea said. "That is understandable given the circumstances."

"I'm scared for the girls." Shan sniffed. "I'm also scared I'll never see my husband again."

"If you'll forgive the intrusive question, why was he not home with you?"

Shan sighed. "He's at the NASA training center in Houston."

"You do realize I have no idea of what you are referring to," Anthea said dryly.

The other woman chuckled. "Sorry. NASA stands for the National Aeronautics and Space Administration. It's an agency of the United States of America, well, my equivalent of the country we're in right now. NASA handle the U.S.'s space missions. Jamal was chosen for the astronaut training program."

"As-tro-naut," Anthea sounded out the word. It sounded terribly similar to two words in the ancient version of the Hellene League of City-States' language. "Star sailor?"

Shan nodded. "The Greek language is the source of the term."

Anthea pulled her legs to her chest and rested her chin on her knees. "I'm beginning to feel as if I don't come from the same world as the rest of you."

"You do." Shan perched on the edge of the bed. "I think the time may be off in your case."

A shiver rippled across Anthea's skin, raising gooseflesh. "What do you mean?"

Shan jumped up and strode to the bedroom door. "Let's go find Bebe and ask to use her computer. A little research may answer our questions."

Anthea scrambled off the bed and followed Shan out to the hallway. "Wait, what's a computer?"

CHAPTER 14

"It's a device to connect to the internet." Shan jogged down the staircase, Anthea on her heels.

"You believe you are explaining things to me," Anthea protested. "But you are not."

Shan glanced over her shoulder as she hit the marble foyer. "It'll be easier to show you."

What's all the shouting about?

Shan jumped at Bebe's voice inside her head. "What the fuck!"

Anthea rested a palm on Shan's shoulder. *Bebe is using silent speech. Shan wishes to borrow a device called a com-pu-ter.*

Goosebumps rose on Shan's arms and legs at the distinct voices inside her head.

I'm in the lab. It's the next door on the left after the infirmary where I checked your eyes. There's a spare laptop in here.

Shan shuddered beneath Anthea's hand. "Do you two have any idea how freaky that is?"

Anthea chuckled. "Forgive us. I've become used to it over the years, as I'm sure Bebe has. However, my chief warden Little Bear would sympathize with you. He also finds silent speech highly uncomfortable."

Shan shook her head. "Lead the way. You've seen more of this house than I have."

She tagged along after Anthea, who strode down the hallway as if she owned the place. Maybe she was used to being in charge.

When they reached the appropriate door, Anthea stared at it in confusion. "Where is the latch?"

Shan examined the door and the panel next to it. The wood veneer was designed to match the other doors in the mansion. The panel was a keypad for entry into the room. One of the buttons on the bottom row was marked "Intercom". She pressed the button. "Bebe? We're outside your lab."

With an electronic hum, a click, and a whoosh, the pneumatic door opened. Poor Anthea jumped backward at what were surely alien sounds to her.

Shan poked her head through the opening. "Is it safe to come in?"

Bebe looked up from her microscope and grinned. "Sure. Just do me a favor and put on slippers." She pointed at the racks of boxes next to the door.

Shan slipped on a pair in her size before she helped Anthea. Sam may have given the priestess the spoken English language, but not the written one.

"What are these slippers for?" Anthea asked as she pulled them over her rather large feet.

"They keep us from contaminating Bebe's lab with dirt, pollen, and so forth," Shan said brightly. "We have a few labs like this where I work for sensitive electronics."

"The goo I collected from your clothes already had a healthy amount of dirt and debris from Otherwhere. But I've been able to separate some of the organic material from Anthea's demons." Bebe made a face. "At least, I think it's organic material."

She blew a curl out of her eyes. "The spare laptop is over on the other desk." She pointed at said desk in the opposite corner of the room. Username is White Rose, and the password is Salem1692 with a capital 'S.'"

"Isn't that rather morbid for a witch?" Shan commented as she crossed to the desk.

"It's a reminder of the stupidity of Normals since not one real witch was executed," Bebe said dryly.

"Understood." Shan smiled to herself as she booted up Bebe's spare laptop.

"Normals?" Anthea couldn't stop staring at all the equipment.

"Anyone who's not a super," Bebe replied.

"Super as in superhero like Aisha?" Poor Anthea looked so lost at all the terms they were throwing at her.

Bebe chuckled. "Super as in supernatural. Witches, weres, vamps, fae."

"Do vampires really exist?" Shan entered the password before she swiveled in the chair to look at Bebe. "I thought you, Sam, and Ptolemy were yanking our chains."

"No, they exist in our universe. But their condition really is a disease." Bebe sighed. "We only recently discovered a cure for it."

"So, how did Ptolemy end up in my alternate universe cousin's body if he was a vampire?" Shan asked.

The doctor stared at the floor. "He died saving my life. His sister shot him."

Well, shit. Shan bit her lower lip. She'd really stepped into an uncomfortable situation.

"The human gods sent him back to aid Sam in her final battle with one of the dinosaur gods, but he no longer had a body." Bebe looked up at Shan. "Our Jake died when a harness snapped while he was doing a high-rise stunt on a movie set."

Shan nodded. "Yeah, that's what happened to my Jake, too."

"The gods repaired the flesh sufficiently to put Ptolemy's spirit into Jake's body," Bebe finished. "It took everyone, including Ptolemy, a little while to get used to the change. As far as anyone outside of this house knows, Jake had some brain damage, which left memory lapses and accounts for the strange accent."

"What about Ptolemy's wife?" Shan asked.

"Tiffany knows the truth since she knew both men, and all of this happened before they got married." Bebe shrugged,

Shan had a feeling there was a lot more to the story, but she didn't want to pry anymore than she already had.

"Th-that's very, very . . . wrong." Anthea wore an alarmed expression. "Restarting the heart or breathing for a drowning victim is one thing. But putting one's spirit into someone else's body—"

"Wait a minute." Shan waved a hand. "You know how to do CPR?"

"CPR?" At least, the question distracted the priestess.

"Cardiopulmonary resuscitation," Bebe said. "When you do chest compressions to trigger the heart to beat on its own—"

"And breathing for someone via the mouth. Yes, of course, I know these techniques." Anthea cocked her head. "Doesn't your version of the Temple of Knowledge include such measures when they teach your young people?"

"I wish more of our people were willing to learn," Bebe admitted.

Shan turned back to the laptop, opened a browser, and typed "the history of CPR" into the search engine. "Anthea, do you know when your Temple of Knowledge started teaching the technique and where it originated?"

"The healers of Kemet recorded using an early form fifteen centuries before the Revelation of Balance, but the current method was developed by a healer in Markanda."

Shan grabbed a pen from a cup on the desk being used as a holder and scribbled the names the priestess gave her on a notepad.

"Kemet is the ancient name for Egypt," Bebe said. "Both my husband and my brother-in-law still call it that because their mother insisted they learn the ancient Egyptian language."

"And Markanda is the ancient name for Samarqand, which is a city in

Uzbekistan." Shan clicked over to the tab with the history of CPR. "Well, I'll be damned. CPR is first mentioned in recovered texts from Egypt's Old Kingdom, and it was modified by a Persian physician from Samarqand."

"Is this Samarqand on the Old Continent?" Anthea asked.

"I'm not sure what you mean by the Old Continent. We need a map," Shan declared as she whirled around on the extra office chair to face the other women.

"It would have to be textured." Anthea scowled. "I have problems reading ink, and I cannot see what you are reading on that plate." She gestured at the laptop.

"Caesar has a globe in his office," Bebe offered. "The mountains and coastlines are raised, but it stops at sea level."

"That may be adequate," Anthea said.

"Let me put my samples away." Bebe busied herself in cleaning up and storing the materials she had been working with before the interruption.

"Let's see if we can narrow down the timeline. You said Balance gave you a thousand years to prepare for the demon invasion, right?" Shan said.

Anthea joined her at the desk. "Yes, the first incursion was the Battle of Toscana in the spring of the one thousand and first year of Balance. It is currently the one thousand-nine hundred and seventy-ninth year of Balance."

"Toscana. Toscana," Shan muttered as she typed. "Tuscany?" She looked up at Anthea. "Did the Roman Empire exist in your world?"

"Roman? As in Roma?" Anthea shook her head. "Roma is small provincial city south of the Toscan capital of Florenza."

"Shan, unplug the laptop and bring it with us." Bebe pressed the button to open the lab door. It hissed as it swung inward. After everyone exited, Bebe made sure it was locked before she led Shan and Anthea back up the hallway.

"Can I ask why you have a full-blown biolab in your house?" Shan asked.

"I keep a small supply of the vaccine and the cure for the V-virus in various locations throughout the western U.S. Not everyone was happy about me discovering the cure." A strong thread of bitterness ran through Bebe's words.

"The resentment of a cure is understandable if this disease gives people the abilities you described over our midday meal," Anthea commented. "Humans like power far too much to give it up willingly."

Shan laughed. "That's true no matter what universe the humans are from."

But the people she'd met so far since she was dragged through the demon's portal seemed willing to help her, Anthea, and Aisha get home. So, things weren't all bad. Maybe that's what Anthea's religion meant by Balance.

CHAPTER 15

Aisha's stomach was thankful Sam chose to drive to the closest department store rather than teleport. However, traffic in this version of Los Angeles was as heavy and slow as that in her own version of the city.

Heck, there was even a homeless man in raggedy clothing on a street corner when Sam braked for a red light. He held up a sign that read, "Re-PeNt for The eNd Is NIgh"

"Some things don't change, do they?" Aisha murmured.

Sam glanced at the homeless guy yelling at the drivers to find their savior. "Except the apocalypse already came and went. All I got was a lousy t-shirt."

"You take the end of the world rather lightly," Aisha said.

The traffic light turned green, and Sam pressed the accelerator on her mid-sized SUV. "I didn't save the world by running around in my underwear."

"I wouldn't be pointing fingers at someone else's outfit, Neo," Aisha shot back.

"Oh, I admit I've had an obsession with Keanu Reeves since I first saw *Bill and Ted's Excellent Adventure*." Sam grinned. "What's your excuse?"

"You sound like my law partner," Aisha grumbled.

"You're an attorney?" Sam glanced at her. "Why on earth would you trade that for being a superhero?"

"I do both. Different people need different types of help."

"Some people need rescuing from a burning building, but others need to collect back child support from their cheating ex-husbands?"

"Actually, yes, they do." Aisha had noticed the baby seat and booster in the back seat of Sam's SUV. "Did your husband cheat?"

Sam burst out laughing. "Oh, hell, no."

"I saw the baby seat," Aisha murmured. "And I recognized the bitter tone in your voice."

"We . . . have our issues just like every other couple." Sam shrugged. "But when you have the responsibilities and powers we do, you've got to be careful about what you teach your kids."

"Believe it or not, my husband and I understand your position," Aisha replied. "We're doing our best to give our son a normal human life."

"Doesn't it make you feel weird playing god?" Sam asked softly. "We can't save everyone."

"Oh, I screwed up a lot when I first started hanging out with the underwear brigade," Aisha admitted.

"Underwear brigade?" Sam chuckled.

"That's what Harri calls us." Aisha laughed. "She's my foster sister as well as my law partner."

"You survived the foster system?"

Aisha's hackles rose. "Oh, because I'm Black I'm the poor little girl getting shuffled from home to home?"

"Some things do not change from universe to universe," Sam grumbled.

Aisha bit her tongue. As much as the blonde's holier-than-thou attitude pissed her off, Aisha still needed Sam's help to return home.

Sam cleared her throat. "I apologize for making an assumption I shouldn't have."

"Apology accepted." After a quarter of a mile crawling through traffic,

Aisha added dryly, "I'm surprised Connie doesn't kick your ass when you pull that kind of shit with her."

Sam emitted a sharp bark of laughter. "All of my family and friends threaten to, except Connie. Our relationship is rather . . . complicated."

"So, she just tattles on you?"

"Yep."

Aisha chuckled. "Sounds just like my baby brother."

"See, your brother went about it the wrong way." Sam smirked. "As the youngest sibling, knowing the older sibling's secrets give you power in the relationship. You don't tattle. You blackmail."

Aisha laughed. "And your sibling didn't resent you for outsmarting them?"

"I think my brother enjoyed being kept on his toes." Sam sobered. "Damn, I miss him."

"I'm sorry," Aisha murmured. "Did you lose him before you became a goddess?"

"After." Sam audibly gulped. "I was so tempted to bring him back. He died the day after his daughter's fourth birthday." She blinked rapidly and sniffed to keep from crying. "Even his ghost said that was the wrong thing to do."

"I depend on my bio and foster siblings to keep my head on straight," Aisha said. "It sounds like you have a similar relationship with Phil and Connie."

"Yeah." Sam swiped at the single tear that managed to escape. "I guess we're both lucky in that regard."

Aisha stared out the passenger window of Sam's SUV. She couldn't imagine having Sam's level of power and not using it to save her siblings' lives.

Aisha pushed a cart and followed Sam and her cart through the women's section of the Arrow Department Store. The death goddess seemed determine to buy anything and everything in hers and Anthea's sizes. When Aisha picked out a pair of athletic shoes to replace the ones Connie had supplied her, Sam yanked them out of Aisha's hands and tossed them in her own cart.

"Let me at least pay for my own clothing," Aisha protested.

Sam lowered her voice. "I appreciate the offer, but think about it. If your credit card isn't declined for being fraudulent, the charges will end up on your counterpart's account. That's not fair to her."

Aisha stared at Sam for a few seconds. "Crap, that didn't even register with me after the two Jakes experience. But I still have cash."

Sam waggled her fingers. "Let me see a bill."

Aisha handed her a twenty.

Sam examined it. "Tubman on the front. That's good." Her right eyebrow rose. "Kal Penn is the Secretary of the Treasury?"

Aisha frowned. "What's wrong with Kal Penn?"

"He's an actor in this universe."

Aisha shrugged. "He was an actor in our universe, too. But he quit Hollywood and worked for Obama during his two terms. Then he was Biden's chief of staff. Now, he's the Secretary of the Treasury under Harris."

"Wow. No shit." Sam handed back the bill. "But you can't spend this here."

Aisha tucked the bill back in her shorts pocket. "I don't like taking someone else's money."

"This isn't charity," Sam retorted as she pushed her cart toward the lingerie section. "Or is public nudity okay where you're from?"

"Nope." Aisha grinned. "You gotta at least wear some colorful underwear."

CHAPTER 16

A text from Bebe flashed on the screen of Sam's SUV, and the computer read it aloud as she drove back to Brentwood.

"It sounds like she and the other ladies have made some headway," Sam commented.

"But why is Anthea being six hundred years off from Shan and me important?" Aisha asked.

"According to her, Balance gave Earth plenty of warning of the demons' invasion." A shiver ran up Sam's spine. "What if they can jump to other dimensions and they're looking for an Earth that's not as prepared?"

Aisha's breath hissed between her teeth. "We don't have witches like the rest of you guys do."

"But you have superheroes," Sam said grimly.

"But we have no idea how to handle these things," Aisha protested. "We accidentally discovered they don't like lightning or water."

"Then we need to pump Anthea for any and all information," Sam said. "I don't want to get caught with my pants down if they come here."

The last thing she needed was another demonic invasion. Thanks to the last one, a crater lake had formed where Mount Rainier used to stand, and everyone in Puget Sound lost their homes and businesses if not their lives.

The coven guards at Bebe and Caesar's estate gave Aisha the evil eye when Sam pulled up to the gate.

"Ms. Ridgeway, you really need to clear unknown guests with Mr. Stanton prior to bringing them to a coven home," Miko Osaka snarled. For her to be that formal, she was pissed as hell.

Which meant Ptolemy had narced when he left to pick up the kids from school.

Sam pursed her lips. It was times like these she really wished Miko's older sister Mai was still stationed in Los Angeles.

Once Sam was calm enough not to launch Miko into orbit, she said, "It was a bit of an emergency at the time. Do you want me to call Alex now?"

"He already knows," Miko bit out. "And you could have taken *your* guests to *your* home."

"Cara Lannigan."

"Master St. James trusts her to keep you safe," Miko snapped.

"And how many times has the bitch shot me?" Sam retorted.

"You deserved it every single time."

"I have half a mind to take you to Pluto and leave you there." Sam ignored the muffled snickers coming from Aisha.

Miko lifted her chin. "With power comes responsibility."

"And you are abusing yours, Ms. Osaka." Sam smiled sweetly. "You want me to tell your boss that, or are you going to let me in?"

Miko signaled for the enforcer inside the guard house to open the gate.

As the spell-reinforced iron slid back on its tracks, Sam lowered her voice. "Just ask Connie on a date and be done with it."

Miko's cheeks flushed beet red, and she stepped back from the driver's side window. "You may enter."

Once they were halfway up the drive, Aisha burst out laughing. "You and Harri would either love each other or kill each other."

"I doubt it would be a real contest," Sam grumbled.

"My girl has taken out some of the deadliest supervillains around, and she has no powers." Aisha grinned. "Against a goddess of Death, I give you even odds."

Sam pulled up in front of the main door and parked. Once they entered the foyer hauling their loot, Sam inclined her head for Aisha to follow her. "I can hear them in Caesar's office."

At the arguing between Shan and Anthea, Sam crossed her fingers Anthea hadn't electrocuted anything because she was damn tired of replacing Caesar's property.

CHAPTER 17

"What do you mean there are two separate land masses?" Standing in the office of Bebe's husband, Anthea traced her finger along the outline of the Old Continent on the globe in front of her. "It's one giant continent. There's no separation. Not even a land bridge like the isthmus between the Long Continents."

"I'm going to give you a crash course on plate tectonics," Shan said.

"I'm still trying to deal with the Panama Canal being built eight centuries ahead of schedule," Bebe muttered from the leather couch.

The office door burst open, and Sam strode into the room with Aisha on her heels. Both of them carried multiple huge bags made from an odd flexible material.

"What the hell are you two bitching about?" Sam demanded.

Anthea crossed her arms. "Shan was about to explain plate tectonics to me."

"And from what we've been able to figure out so far, we think Anthea comes from the mid-fifteenth century," Bebe added.

"Whoa." Aisha's expression grew concerned. "Do we need to worry about changing her future? Like breaking the Temporal Prime Directive?"

"This isn't *Star Trek*," Sam snapped.

"If Shan's Many-Worlds theory is correct, whatever information you reveal to me, and I act upon, will cause my timeline to split and create another alternate world," Anthea said. "Not to mention, you haven't shown me much my world doesn't have other than Bebe's incredibly fast miniature oven and your self-moving wagons." She picked up her cup she'd left on the desk when she examined the globe. "You even have Jing black tea."

"Our priestess is a caffeine addict." Bebe smiled wryly. "I wouldn't introduce her to Starbucks or Timmie's if I were you, Sam."

"Explaining this would be easier if I had a globe I could take apart." Shan scratched the top of her head.

"Wait. I've got an idea." Sam set her bags on the floor next to the couch.

Anthea sipped her tea while she observed their antics. They seemed to regard her as uneducated idiot. Normally, such behavior would elicit a storm of anger. Maybe her sessions with High Sister Mya of Child were more effective in dealing with her childhood issues than she thought.

Sam closed her eyes, and a model of the World appeared in the middle of the room. A globe Anthea could see. She reached out with her free hand, and her fingers passed through the sphere.

"It's made of light," Anthea whispered.

"A hologram." Shan's voice was filled with awe. "Without a projector."

"It's just a glamour, ladies," Bebe teased.

"And I'm the projector," Sam added. "You want the standard classroom three-quarter view, Shan?"

"Yes, please."

A vertical quarter of the sphere disappeared. The interior vaguely resembled the inside of a peach. But were the colors correct?

"Is there really an iron and nickel core in the middle of the World?" Anthea asked.

A pleased smile crossed Sam's face though her eyes remained closed.

"Yes." Shan ran through the other different layers and their composition.

Anthea stared in amazement. "A magnetic field on such a giant level that it protects the entire World. Fascinating."

"What?" Shan's startled expression would have been amusing under other circumstances.

"You're the one who said what we call light is on an electromagnetic spectrum." Anthea gestured at the image with her free hand. "If melted steel can affect a nearby compass while the liquid is being stirred, it only stands to reason that the World's outer core would produce the same effect on a much larger scale."

"What do you mean by protecting the World?" Bebe asked.

"If the sun produces light both I and everyone else can see, it stands to reason the sun produces other types of energy, like the microwaves in Bebe's miniature oven." Anthea shrugged. "If those rays are harmful to living flesh as you said microwaves are, then logically, the World's magnetic field would block most of them, else our bodies would be heated to the point our blood boiled the instant we stepped outside, instead of merely receiving a bad burn on exposed skin if we are in sunlight too long."

"Holy crap!" Sam shook her head. "You are going to get along great with my sister-in-law. You talk just like her." She made the globe one piece again, but with Shan's plates outlined.

Anthea cocked her head and frowned while she studied the revised map. "So you deem the Stone Belt Mountains a dividing line between the western and eastern sections of the Old Continent?"

"Yes, what we call the Urals were created about the same time as the Appalachians." Shan pointed to the Smoky Mountains. "The Urals or Stone Belt Mountains sit upon a thicker part of the earth's crust, so they don't show the same erosion—"

"As the Great Smokey Mountains. That makes sense." Anthea nodded until she realized the other four women were staring at her. "What?"

"Do you call all of the Appalachian Mountains the Smokey Mountains?" Aisha asked as she traced the line of peaks.

Anthea nodded again. "Why?"

Aisha drew a circle with her finger around a section near the south end of the chain. "We generally only refer to this subsection as the Great Smokey Mountains." She grinned. "Nice to know we share some of the same names."

"I do have a question." Anthea pointed to the outline of the Peaceful Sea. "All of the places where these plates meet are known for their volcanic activity and ground quakes. However, the islands that form the Kingdom of O'ahu all have volcanoes on them, and they are nowhere near the edge of a plate." She turned to Shan. "Is it safe to assume the islands formed because there's a thin spot in the crust?"

Shan grinned as if Anthea were a prized pupil. "Very good. If your time-line were the same as ours, you'd be teaching at MIT or working for NASA."

"I'm not sure if I would like flying," Anthea said.

"Are you joking? It's the greatest thing in the world." Aisha laughed. "It's even better when you can do it on your own power."

"I will accept your word for it." Anthea inclined her head.

"So where do you come from?" Aisha asked.

"Do you mind if we use the perfectly serviceable globe in the room?" Sam said.

"Poor baby," Bebe mocked. "Are you getting tired?"

"No." The light version of the world faded, and Sam blinked. "I don't want to accidentally blind Anthea because my still human concentration failed."

A tingle swept over Anthea's skin, and the physical globe and its stand slid to the middle of the room without anyone touching it. She eyed Sam. "Is there any talent you do not have?"

"Knowing when to keep her mouth shut," Bebe teased.

Anthea chuckled while she spun the globe to her side of the Northern Long Continent. "Here is Issura." She used her finger to trace the queendom based on the raised coastline. "The Duchy of Orrin is now the southern-most duchy of Issura with the loss of Tandor to a demon army last year."

"If you're six centuries behind us, it explains the Chumash words in your native language," Sam said. "They would have controlled that area."

"Wait a minute." Aisha stared at the globe. "The states are wrong."

"What do you mean wrong?" Sam asked.

"Where's Mojave?"

"The Mojave Desert is in the same place it is in my world," Shan offered.

"I mean the State of Mojave." Aisha circled a portion of the globe. "It should be here. It's like New Mexico and Texas ate my home state."

"How many states do you have?" Sam asked.

"Fifty-four," Aisha stated.

"Fifty-four?" Shan gave her a puzzled look.

"Besides missing Mojave, Pennsylvania and New York haven't split like Virginia did. Then, there's Puerto Rico." Aisha shrugged.

Shan looked at Sam. "Fifty?"

"Fifty." Sam nodded. "Though I am curious. Did Pennsylvania and New York split during the Civil War?"

Aisha shook her head. "Pennsylvania split into Pennsylvania and West Pennsylvania during the Whiskey Rebellion."

Sam laughed. "That's one of the few things you've said that makes sense."

"New York split into North York and New York after the *Amistad* uprising." Aisha folded her arms across her chest. "From the looks on your faces, Puerto Rico still isn't a state here."

"No," Sam said. "When did it become a state in your universe?"

"1968," Aisha answered.

"The '67 referendum passed?" Sam whistled. "That's amazing."

"Anthea, does your country do a lot of trading with Asia?" Shan asked. "Is that how you learned, um, Jing?"

Anthea's mouth quirked. "There's a long story behind me learning the Jing language, but they produce the powder we use in mining."

"And flash bangs?" Shan teased.

"And flash bangs," Anthea admitted.

"Is that how you understood her before Sam messed with her brain?" Aisha asked.

"Sam!" Bebe glared at the goddess.

"All I did was give instant knowledge of English to her," Sam retorted. "We didn't have time for Shan's laborious translation efforts."

"Hey!" Shan propped her fists on her hips.

"You were doing just fine," Aisha consoled the other woman.

"Actually, it was Ptolemy who figured out Anthea was speaking Middle Mandarin," Shan admitted. "It's why she and I could sort of understand each other before you gave her modern English. I thought he was lying about being over two thousand years old, but the two of them rattled on so fast, I couldn't understand them."

"But how did the Chumash add Old English and Latin to the mix of their language?" Sam asked.

"Show me the places where these languages come from in your worlds," Anthea said.

Aisha spun the globe back to the Old Continent. "The British Isles is where most of the language we speak came from. Old English is the version of our language from what is for you ten centuries ago.

"Latin is even older." Aisha pointed to the lower part of the boot of Toscana. "It can be traced back twenty-two centuries before your time. Even our English has many words with their roots in Latin because of the Roman Empire's invasion of England."

Anthea chuckled. "So, what I call Albion is home of the queen with the furry corgi dogs?"

"Yep." Bebe grinned.

Anthea sobered. "My Roma never achieved the prominence yours did. Any invasion of one nation by another was dealt with by the Temples."

"How?" Sam asked.

"Sadly, through assassination of the power-hungry head of state if they didn't respond to other means." Anthea sighed. "When the queens and Temples of Albion and Eire were faced with total defeat by invading demon armies, they evacuated as many of their people to the mainland as they could before they triggered the Temple of Death's last resort spells.

"Some refugees from the Briton Diaspora settled in what became Issura, as did younger nobles and tradespeople from Toscana. They joined with the surviving Chumash after the Battle of Apache Tears."

"What is the Battle of Apache Tears?" Sam asked.

Anthea had to sip some tea to wet her suddenly dry mouth. "Four centuries ago, the entire Apache Empire sacrificed themselves in the Valley of the Lost to keep a demon army from flooding across the Great Plains. Only a handful of children and one of their priests of Knowledge survived."

"D-didn't the Britons return to the islands once the demons were dead?" Shan appeared as if she were about to purge her midday meal.

"They cannot." Anthea shook her head, her own stomach rebelling at the memory of her similar actions in Tandor. "No one can step onto any of the islands without dying themselves."

"Sounds like using a nuke," Sam mused.

"A what?" For all the worth of Sam's gift of her language, Anthea wished she'd added the definitions of her English words as well.

"It's a device that replicates the power of the sun on a small scale." Aisha appeared as sad as Sam.

Frustration gnawed in Anthea's nerves, but before she said something she regretted, Shan offered a better explanation.

"Think of your flashbangs as an expression of explosive power. One flashbang equals the power to kill one demon."

Anthea suppressed the urge to laugh. "It usually takes more than one."

Shan made an impatient face. "Fine. Three. Now, add ten zeroes after that three."

Anthea blinked as she ran through to the logical conclusion. The other four women looked especially somber. "You don't have a Temple of Death, but you have that kind of power?"

None of the women would face her. They all took a great interest in the carpet.

"And you use it against other humans?" That idea bothered Anthea the most. It scarred her soul when so many people died trying to stop the demons at Tandor. Worst of all was losing Bertrice, her counterpart at the Orrin Temple of Death, during that battle. But there was a reason that chain of spells were referred to as Death's Last Resort. But to use that level of power against innocents?

She swallowed the judgment threatening to erupt from her. "I think I need some more tea."

CHAPTER 18

Shan may not have powers like everyone else in the room, but she didn't need supernatural abilities to sense Anthea's shock and disappointment in the rest of them. The emotion lingered long after the priestess left the office, shutting the door behind her.

"How dare she?" Pink flooded Sam's cheeks.

"No," Bebe said. "We're upset because she's right."

"I'll go talk to her." Shan took two steps before Aisha laid a hand on her shoulder.

"Give Anthea a chance to cool off," the superhero murmured. "It sounds like she grew up in a pretty rigid environment compared to ours."

Shan whirled to face the taller woman. "Rigid? Maybe she has the right to the moral high ground. The humans of her world aren't killing each other in stupid wars with the most awful weapons ever devised!"

She charged out of the office and head down the hall toward the kitchen.

Anthea is out by the pool, Sam said inside Shan's head.

Shan pivoted and headed to the opposite end of the house. That damn telepathy thing was really beginning to piss her off. Grandmother Wong didn't pull crap like that.

Ironically, Grandmother Wong would object to Anthea's culture of absolute service. She snuck Grandfather Wong and what was left of his family out of China. They were a family of scholars, something not really tolerated by the current government.

Shan's pace slowed as she reached the French doors overlooking the patio. What exactly could she say to make things better? Maybe it was more important to try and fail. She opened the right door and stepped outside.

Yep, they were definitely in sunny California. Not a cloud in the sky and the light glinted along the surface of the crystal blue water. Anthea sat on the edge of the concrete with her legs dangling in the pool.

"Can I get you a towel, ma'am?"

Shan jumped at the cracking voice. A teenage boy stepped out from behind a plant. His pale legs and freckles explained why he stayed under the awning. He swiped glossy black bangs out of his eyes.

"Um, no, thanks." Shan glanced at Anthea, who had to have known she was speaking to the teenager, but she didn't turn to look at Shan.

She looked at the boy once again. "Are you spying on her?"

"No." He scowled at Shan. "I offered her a towel. Then I tried to entertain her by making water animals. She's as moody as the next-door neighbor."

"Do you work here?" she asked.

"Only during the summer." He grinned. "Cleaning Cousin Bebe's pool is way better than working for my dad in a freakin' hot kitchen." His expression turned wry. "Then she asked me to stick around when the neighbor popped in with . . ." His cheeks turned crimson beneath the peach fuzz.

"Uninvited guests?" Shan volunteered.

"Uh, yeah." He stared at his bare feet on the glazed terra cotta tiles of the patio.

"Can I ask you a question?"

His head jerked up. "Depends."

Shan decided to charge ahead. "Why don't you say the name of the blond lady inside the house, and why is she careful not to say any other deity's name?"

"Actually, that's two questions," he teased before he turned serious. "Saying her name is like praying to her, and frankly, it makes her and all the supernaturals a little uncomfortable." He shrugged. "I mean, you're not supposed to know your goddess, right?"

Shan wasn't sure how to answer. She didn't think the kid would appreciate who her grandmother was, nor did she want to discuss her lineage with strangers. Secondly, the kid didn't look like a vampire, but then she hadn't met one other than Ptolemy, who was now in a human body. How would she know if she had? Besides, the kid probably stayed under the awning because he'd combust with any sunscreen less than SPF 100.

So, she nodded and said, "And the answer to my second question?"

"The gods only speak each other's names if they want the other's attention."

Aisha was right. Rival pantheons yelling each other's names would be equivalent to rival gangs calling out each other. That could get messy quick.

"By the way, I'm Shan Wong-Washington." She smiled and held out her palm.

"Leonard Epstein." He shook her hand. "You sure there's not anything I can get you, Shan?"

"No, thank you." She crossed to the pool, the baking concrete scorching her bare soles every step of the way, and sat down next to Anthea. Shan dipped her right foot in the sparkling water. Refreshingly chill. She lowered both legs until the waves lapped just below her knees.

"I owe you and the others an apology," Anthea said softly. "It's not my place to judge the morals of your worlds. I know so little of them."

"Honestly, I think we could use a judge that's willing to slap us upside the head for being stupid." Shan sighed. "If it's any consolation, no one in my world takes nuclear weapons lightly."

"But what will happen to my world if we defeat the demons?" Anthea shook her head. "I'm only a justice, and I see the evil humans do to each other every day. Despite the Temples' efforts in mental and emotional care and the war for our very survival, humans still rob, assault, and even murder other humans. From your comments and the others', my world is further along than we should be. And understanding the results of your worlds, I fear the consequences of winning our war."

"Or your people could reach for the stars." Shan gestured at the sky. "Explore the depths of the oceans. Maybe you strive to be better than we are." She smiled at Anthea. "Maybe we should be striving to be more like you."

The priestess finally looked at Shan. "You remind me quite a bit of Lady Shi Hua. She is unfailingly positive no matter what trouble we have found ourselves in. I hope neither of you lose that relish of life."

"You'll see her soon."

"Even when I return home and after her husband is crowned as the emperor of Jing, I will probably never see her again." Anthea kicked at the water, sending a flash of sparkling droplets into the air.

"Things can change, Chief Justice." Shan climbed to her feet, and the chlorinated water made dark rings on the concrete as it dripped down her legs. "If there's anything I've learned in my lifetime is that things can change if we have the courage to change them."

CHAPTER 19

Aisha was laying out an outfit on the bed Anthea had been using when the priestess strode into the room.

"Oh." She paused, glancing at the covers Aisha had straightened before spreading Sam's purchases for Anthea on the comforter. "Are we to be sharing quarters? I apologize for leaving the room in disarray."

Aisha waved away the other woman's amends with one hand as she matched crew socks. It was too dang hot in L.A. to be wearing more than socks that end just over the ankle bone. "No worries, girl. I'm sure you have staff for that sort of thing."

"I do not ask Sivan to do basic tasks I can handle myself," Anthea snapped.

Aisha straightened. She'd hit the priestess's pet peeve, and it took her a second to realize what it was.

"I apologize for any misunderstanding. I meant it's nice to see a sister who's done well in the world. I wasn't trying to step on your toes. I thought you might need some help with our style of clothing."

Anthea closed her eyes, took a deep breath, and slowly released it. Aisha recognized the relaxation technique.

The priestess opened her blood-colored eyes. "It is my turn to atone. I don't like showing weakness. However, I must rely on Sivan for such tasks as cosmetics and hair styling." She looked away for a moment before she eyed Aisha again. "I should not aim my anger at my own shortcomings toward you. I am sorry."

Aisha chuckled and held up her palms. "Let's stop there, or we'll be apologizing to each other all night. Let's also assume no one is trying to insult anyone, and go from there. Besides, my brother helps me with my cosmetics and hair, so I can't talk."

She waved at the clothes on the comforter. "I know our styles and fabrics are a lot different than what you're used to."

The priestess smirked. "Shan explained superheroes to me. You don't wear bright colors like the ones in her universe do."

Being called dull felt like a slam, but Anthea seemed to have Harri's sarcastic sense of humor. Unfortunately, her word choices reminded Aisha of the snotty kids at school. Seems the priestess wasn't the only one who needed to get a chip off her shoulder.

"I thought you didn't see colors the way the rest of us do."

"I don't." Anthea's smile turned genuine. "Your outfit's style is similar to our wardens. One necessary to fight in. I rather like the idea of using the natural hues of your namesake."

"You actually have ghost owls?"

"The Valley of the Lost and Diné have them." The priestess appeared lost in a memory. "My father and half-siblings took me to see them hunt when I was in Diné last fall."

"Diné? They are a sovereign country in your time?"

"Of course."

"And you're part Diné?"

"Three-quarters," Anthea said proudly.

"Are the Diné matrilineal in your universe?"

"Yes."

Aisha perched in the edge of the bed. "How did you end up in a Chumash nation?"

Anthea joined her and explained how talented children were claimed by the nation-state of where it was first learned the child had magic abilities. In her great-grandmother's case, complications with her pregnancy forced her to stay in Issura until she birthed her daughter. Females born blind were considered to be touched by the goddess and automatically claimed by the Temple of Balance.

"I wish my dad was here." Amazement didn't even begin to cover what Aisha felt. "He taught Native American history at Canyon Pointe University and now at Morehouse College."

"Your father is—" Anthea paused, obviously trying to find the right words in English. "—a civilian intellectual?"

"We call them professors, but yeah." Aisha smiled while she talked about her family's history in Atlanta, and the summers she spent with her dad at archeological digs in the American Southwest, Mexico, and Central America. Anthea listened raptly, offering her own perspective since she was living in times Dad studied his whole life.

Anthea shook her head with an amazed expression. "How did your schools of advanced learning start without a Temple of Knowledge to draw from? Even the University of Issura was founded by Reverend Father Mugu of Knowledge in conjunction with Prince Consort Pismo."

"If it makes you feel better, some universities and colleges in my universe were founded by religious leaders, too. Morehouse started in the basement of a Baptist church—"

A knock on the partially open door interrupted her. Sam poked her head around the edge.

"My sister-in-law texted the all-clear." She frowned. "You two have been up here for over an hour, and Anthea isn't even dressed yet?"

"My fault." Aisha jumped to her feet. "I asked her about her version of Navajo and Chumash history, and we lost track of time."

Sam shook her head and smiled. "I'm not the one trapped in an alternate universe. The rest of us will be in the living room." She pulled the door shut as she left.

Anthea held up a pair of tan denim shorts trimmed in matching lace. "Why is there metal teeth so close to your genitalia on this garment? Does your society enjoy pain with their pleasure?"

Aisha bit the side of her cheek to keep from laughing and proceeded to show Anthea how zippers and Velcro worked.

CHAPTER 20

In Bebe's living room, Sam stopped pacing and tapped the toe of her right foot impatiently.

"You need to chill before you crack the slab," Phil said crossly from her chair. "Not everyone can change their clothing with a thought like you can."

"You can do it, too," Sam shot back.

"I spent five thousand years doing it the old fashioned way," Phil said dryly.

Shan and Bebe giggled on the couch.

"And it's not like Ptolemy hasn't taken care of the kids without us," Phil added.

"That's part of what I'm afraid of," Sam said sourly. "If he lets Billy have too much soda, I'll be the one to deal with him bouncing off the walls all night and cranky before school in the morning from the withdrawals."

"You can call Duncan," Bebe said. "You know he'd teleport home for a little bit to help."

"And admit I can't handle my own son?" Sam snorted. "No thanks."

"Does Billy have your abilities?" Shan asked.

"Not so far." Sam dropped into the free armchair. "But the potential's there. Why?"

"My dad doesn't have my grandmother's abilities, nor do I." The younger woman shrugged. "But since my grandmother is Kwan Yin, and Jamal is descended from Lugh, we wonder what we might be accidentally setting on the world if we have kids."

Sam rolled her eyes. "I don't know what to tell you because I should never have been able to get pregnant according to my witch doctor."

Bebe grabbed a pillow from behind her and launched it at Sam's face. She snagged the pillow before it hit.

"What have I said about calling me that?" Bebe growled.

"If you were that offended, you would have thrown a fireball at me instead of a bag of polyester fluff." Sam tossed the pillow far more gently back to Bebe.

"She can throw fireballs?" Anthea asked as she and Aisha entered the room.

Sam smiled to herself. Anthea looked really good in the tan denim shorts and the burgundy sleeveless button-down. The outfit set off her skin tone and black, glossy hair.

"It could be worse." Sam pushed to her feet. "She's been known to stab gods in the ass with a hypo full of elephant tranquilizers."

"Those clothes look awesome on you, Anthea," Shan said cheerfully.

"I feel naked," the priestess grumbled.

"What are you talking about?" Sam threw her hands in the air. "The Chumash wore skirts and belts—"

"And if Anthea's time correlates to our mid-fifteenth century, it's the middle of the Little Ice Age," Aisha said. "It would explain her heavier clothing though she lives in California."

"Ignore them," Shan waved her hand. "You look fabulous."

Anthea looked down at her top. "My breasts should not stick out to this degree. However, I do need to blend in your populace."

"Where's her shades?" Sam asked. She'd grabbed them at Arrow because they didn't have time to mess with contacts. And laying a glamour on the priestess would only attract the wrong kind of attention while they were at Cal Tech.

"Here." Aisha held up the glasses.

"What in Balance is that?" Anthea leaned away from the spectacles in Aisha's hand.

"Technically, they're sunglasses," Aisha said. "They're used to protect your eyes from those dangerous solar rays. In your case, it's to hide your pretty red peepers."

"Bebe mentioned them earlier. How do I use them?"

Aisha showed her how to put them on.

"We may have a problem with this plan." Anthea reached up with her right index finger and tapped the lens in front of her right eye. "These totally block my vision."

"Aw, shit!" Sam rubbed her forehead. "I'm sorry. I wasn't thinking."

"It is all right." Anthea removed the sunglasses. "I assume these work like the glass panes in windows, and you can see through them."

"We can't tell anyone you cast a spell yourself." Sam crossed her arms and resumed tapping her right toes on the shag carpet.

"I generally do not bother telling anyone anything about me." Beneath Anthea's grimace was a layer of sadness. "Humans prefer to make up their own tales, regardless of the truth."

"You've got to understand something, Anthea." Bebe smirked. "Sam is probably the most and least intelligent person you will ever meet."

Time to retaliate. Sam smiled as she pulled a couple of bills from her jeans pocket. "By the way, our pizza order from Anthony's will be here around seven. It's already paid for, but here's the tip for the delivery driver."

The doc sighed in exasperation. "Is there a reason, besides pissing off Miko, why you can't order pizza to your own house?"

"Because I told Ptolemy to take Tony and Cleo to my house for a sleepover." Sam's smile shifted to a full-on grin. "And you have more guest bedrooms than I do at the moment."

"It would have been nice if you informed me." Bebe scowled at her. "Did you bother to warn Connie?"

Sam lifted her chin. "Yes, I did. So there." She forced herself to calm down. "Look, Bebe, I need you to continue your investigation into these fucking demons. It sounds like magic is the only thing besides water and lightning that keeps these monsters at bay in Anthea's universe. We need to be ready if they come here. This situation isn't governed by some stupid prophecy like me and the dino demons."

Bebe stared at her. "You're right." She stood and started to leave the room before she whirled to face the group again. "And I really, really hate having to admit you are right." She stomped out of the living room and down the hallway.

"Geez, girl." Aisha shook her head. "Do you have to take all of Harri's worst attributes?"

"Except your Harri can't literally make you do shit you don't want to, can she?" Phil rose.

"Despite her lack of powers, she does a hell of a job getting everyone in the Lechuza Building to obey her." Aisha's wry smile said everything.

"You have a building named after your superhero moniker?" Sam shook her head. "Why don't you put up a huge sign on the roof saying 'Batcave Here' with a big arrow pointing down?"

A frosty expression spread across Aisha's face. "First of all, it's the Owl's Nest. I don't need DC-Warner Brothers' legal department breathing down my neck. Second, my predecessor's idiotic family were the ones who named the building, not me. And third, I need a place to unwind after nearly getting killed, and I can't take my fear and jitters out on my son."

"I get it," Sam said quietly. "After collecting souls, I usually go to Pluto to get my head on straight before I go home."

"Pluto?" Shan's eyes grew big and round. "Please tell me we're talking Disneyland."

Phil smirked. "Ask her what she did to the planet before the Kuiper Explorer did its fly-by a few years ago."

No one needed to hear that story. "We need to get to the lab." Sam held out her hands. "Let's go."

Even though the other ladies joined hands, Shan still asked, "What did she do? Write 'Kilroy was here' in large enough letters for the probe to see?"

"No, she painted the heart formation—"

Sam twisted time and space, aiming for Pasadena. The teleport didn't stop Phil at all.

"—neon pink."

"Ohmigod! What did the folks at NASA say?" Shan laughed.

"They assumed it was a problem with the Kuiper's camera," Tiffany said. Her reading glasses were perched on the end of her nose, but below her lab coat, she wore fishnet stockings and black biker boots with silver chains. Real silver. Knowing her, she had her silver knives tucked inside the boots. Once an enforcer, always an enforcer.

"This is my sister-in-law Tiffany Stephens," Sam said.

"Doctor Tiffany Stephens," she said sharply.

Sam ignored the jibe and introduced her little cadre from different universes.

"So, you are a physician like Bebe?" Anthea said as she shook Tiffany's hand.

Tiffany chuckled. "No one's a doctor like Bebe."

Sam pulled out her phone and texted Ares to let him know she and her group were at Tiffany's lab. With a soft pop of displaced air, he appeared next to his granddaughter. Anthea didn't so much as wince when he appeared. Sam breathed a sigh of relief. It was nice when another deity listened to her once in a while.

"How are you, Cherry Blossom?" He gave Tiffany a bear hug.

"I'm great, Grandpa Ares." She returned his affectionate embrace.

"And my favorite daughter?" He turned to Phil.

"You are so full of bullshit." But she laughed and gave him a hug.

"Samantha." He inclined his head like he always did. No attempted hug now that she could kick his ass to the next galaxy.

But his dark eyes literally lit up when he spotted her three guests. "And who might you lovely ladies be?"

Sam stepped between him and her wayward sisters. "Don't even think about it, Ares."

"Why are you assuming I would act untoward to your friends?" he protested.

"Grandpa, do you really want us to talk to Bebe?" Tiffany said slyly.

He paled. "That won't be necessary, Cherry Blossom."

Sam went through introductions and explained the situation of her guests and the strange silicon demons in Otherwhere.

"Other universes?" He stroked his black beard. "No, I haven't heard of such things. These demons though are worrisome. While it relieves me the denizens of Otherwhere find them tasty, I would prefer not to go another round with shapeshifting foes."

"Yeah, something tells me Olympian bronze would be useless on these bastards." Sam turned to Tiffany. "Any bright ideas on how to match these ladies with their respective universes?"

"If my idea works, I can calculate their quantum vibration compared to ours." She tapped her chin as she stared at one of her machines. "The problem will be finding the universe with the matching number." She looked up at Sam. "I know you want to help them get home, but we have no idea what will happen to our universe if you leave it."

Sam closed her eyes and rubbed the bridge of her nose. "Explain it to me like I'm Ellie and I'm still in kindergarten."

Tiffany cocked her head. "You want me to actually show you film of Galloping Gertie?"

"You think Sam could cause self-replicating harmonic resonance in another universe?" Shan asked.

Sam gritted her teeth. Was everyone in here smarter than she was?

"It makes sense," Anthea commented. "Even though she is one of many, any one of your versions of Death comprise a large part of your universe."

"So, if Tiffany popped up in one of our universes, it would be like a single drop of rain," Aisha said. "And Sam would be a freakin' hurricane."

"Exactly. You three are here, and our universe is still stable. As far as we know, anyway. By the way, Aisha, you can say 'fuck' here." Tiffany grinned. "My fucking students say it all the fucking time."

Aisha smiled sweetly in return. "I also have a four-year-old who repeats everything he hears."

"Been there. Done that," Tiffany answered. "Has he flushed things down the toilet that aren't supposed to get flushed?"

"Yeah." Aisha snickered. "Our building manager Miguel had to take apart our bathroom to get the Pooh bear out of the plumbing."

Sam rolled her eyes. When she had Billy and Maxine, she wasn't this obsessive about their influences. And she was rather proud to be the one to teach her kids the appropriate use of curse words. "Tiffany, please use your ambassadorial manners and test my friends for their quantum vibration, instead of the issues of toilet training."

"Have you taken readings for your universe?" Shan asked.

Tiffany laughed. "What do you think grad students are for?"

Sam crossed her fingers that Tiffany could give her a clue of where Aisha, Shan, and Anthea belonged. Otherwise, the collective sarcasm and wisecracks might drive her insane. She got more than enough from her own family and friends.

CHAPTER 21

Anthea tried to keep her breathing even, and her eyes closed, while the machine she stood in made the most peculiar humming. Her skin tingled, very similar to the sensation of Luc or Shi Hua performing a Light spell while she was present. In a way, it made sense because their level of scientific advancement was almost like magic.

Tiffany couldn't do anything about the low-level infrared light her machine gave off. The sight wasn't painful like the first time Anthea saw Sam. More like entering the Temple of Balance's kitchen shortly before the Winter Solstice when their cook Deborah baked up a storm before the holiday. The oven would be so hot it glowed a light pink. Anthea had to squint when she entered the kitchen to filch an almond pastry or two.

The humming died, and the tingling sensation faded. Anthea opened her right eye. Everything looked relatively normal again. The door to the machine opened.

"How are you feeling?" Tiffany asked with a note of concern.

"I am quite all right." Anthea gave the smaller woman a reassuring smile. "Is it safe for me to leave your device?"

Tiffany stepped back. "We're all done."

Anthea stepped out of the machine. Sam, Ares, and Phil stood on the other side of the room, whispering in a language Anthea didn't recognize.

She turned to Tiffany. "Should I ask?"

"They think they're being sneaky." Tiffany made a disgusted face. "Stupid fucking gods."

Anthea raised her right eyebrow.

"Don't give me that holier-than-thou look," Tiffany grumbled. "It didn't work with the minister who did my first wedding. It's not going to work now."

Anthea glanced at the trio in the corner. "At least, your deities speak to you. The only time Balance spoke to me, she told me to jump off a cliff."

Tiffany started to laugh, but she stopped abruptly. "You're not joking, are you? Did you jump?"

"Dragging my youngest brother all the way down." Anthea looked away from the shorter woman for a moment. She feared she may never see her father or her siblings ever again. But even Bumblebee had laughed once they were fished out of the sea. And he jumped not knowing how to swim. She'd made a point of teaching him once they safely returned to Orrin.

"The incident is still humorous." Anthea smirked. "You are allowed to laugh."

"Well—" Tiffany grinned. "In all fairness, Sam has told me to do some anatomically impossible things."

"May I ask why?"

"She hates it when I'm right." Tiffany pulled a small metal ring from her pocket with a number of what appeared to be keys on it. "I need to calculate the measurements and do some comparisons. I've got drinks and snacks in my office. Sam!"

"What!"

"Show some manners and entertain *your* guests in my office!" Tiffany threw the ring of keys in Sam's direction.

"Yes, Miss Tiffany," Sam said in an exaggerated servile tone as she caught the flying metal bits.

Tiffany's grandfather crossed to the small woman, but his attention was totally on Anthea. He extended his arm. "May I escort you to Cherry Blossom's office, Chief Justice?"

"Why?" Anthea frowned. According to the other ladies, Ares was one of their equivalents of Conflict.

He seemed nonplussed by her blunt answer, but then, most people were. However, neither he nor Sam were what Anthea expected of a deity.

"Um, well, I was trying to be polite."

Behind him, Sam and Phil were leaning on each other as they struggled to contain their humor.

"Except you did not make the same offer to any of the other women here," Anthea pointed out. "Therefore, I am assuming you have an ulterior motive." For Love's sake, Luc did a better job the first time he seduced her.

Ares's ingratiating smile was back. "The other women are not as lovely as you are, m'lady."

"I may not see the same way the rest of you do, but I know damn well my nose is too large to be considered conventionally attractive. Would you like to try again?"

"Whoever told you that should be flogged," Ares stated.

"Not to mention, normally, the adherents of Balance are not allowed to have intimate relationships." Anthea folded her arms across her chest.

"You said normally?" He cocked his head and gave her what she assumed was supposed to be a flirtatious smile. "Under what circumstances can you have an . . . intimate relationship?"

"Only to procreate."

"Grandpa Ares," Tiffany drawled with a warning tone. "Stop now while you're still behind."

"But if dear Anthea needs children, I should endeavor to assist her in her plight," he protested.

Anthea shook her head. The god was amusing, but it was like her verbal sparring with Crown Prince Po. Entertaining, but nothing could come of it.

"Lord Ares, I don't know about the gods in this plane, but in mine, a deity's words have power. Do yours?"

"Of course." He took her sword hand in both of his.

She quashed the urge to jab him in the nose with her other hand. And her own gods wouldn't grant her wish that she were a mover in the next three heartbeats.

"How are you going to create a new womb for me?" She stepped closer. "Not even my gods can do that." She could feel everyone's attention, and her own fury at her circumstances came roaring back to life.

"And why do you sully your honor by playing the fool?" Anthea gestured at the other women of his plane with her free hand. "Both Sam and Tiffany asked you to mind your manners. But not your own daughter. Because she knew you would disregard her words and her emotions, just as you did your granddaughter's."

Ares' mouth dropped open, and he stared at her through her diatribe. Not with anger. No, it was surprise coupled with . . . respect?

"I know you can kill me with a thought." Anthea lifted her chin. "I would prefer you simply do it now, so I don't have to endure any more of your hurtful offers. Because all I want right at this moment is to go home."

"I beg your forgiveness." Ares released her hand and inclined his head. "I never meant to reopen the wounds of your soul. As recompense, I shall do what is in my power to aid you and your companions in your quest for your homes."

"Let's go get snacks." Sam's words weren't a command, but Anthea stepped around Ares and followed this variation of Death toward the main exit of Tiffany's workshop.

Anthea shoved her hands into the pockets of her short leggings. Maybe it was a good thing her gods didn't interact with humans like they did here. Her temper probably would have resulted in her death long before now.

CHAPTER 22

Shan giggled at the expression on Anthea's face as she took her first ever sip of cola.

The priestess finally swallowed. "The prickly sensation is rather unique."

"Bubbles make the beverage," Aisha said.

"Oooo! We should introduce Anthea to bubble tea next!" Shan popped a Dorito into her mouth.

"How long are you planning on staying here?" Sam sat another round of soda cans and snacks on the coffee table.

The anxiety swept over Shan again. "Thanks, I managed to forget our real problems for all of a minute."

"I'm sorry for shitting on you, Shan." Sam crossed to Tiffany's desk, wheeled the office chair over to the sitting area where the rest were munching on chips and nuts, and dropped into the ergonomically correct seat. "Ares thinks we should consult with the Fates."

Shan chewed and swallowed her chip. "How are your Fates going to help us?"

"Whether you call them the Moirae, the Norns, or Ma'at, the Grey Ladies are beyond what you consider gods," Ares said around a mouthful of potato chips. "Even my father fears angering them. I cannot guarantee their assistance, but they have a vested interest in making things right in this universe."

"And what if their vested interest is simply killing us to fix the problem?" Aisha asked.

"That's why I'll be going with you." Sam reached for a Twinkie and ripped open the cellophane.

"But going to these Fates' realm cannot be as easy as walking to their gates, knocking politely, and requesting their help." Anthea took another tentative sip of her cola.

"In every story Grandmother Wong ever told me, the protagonist is tested in some way, or they have to fool the entity," Shan said.

"Look, I've made a few calls to some other friends." Sam licked the vanilla crème from the corner of her mouth. "Not even Norman has a better suggestion of what to do to get you three home."

"What if Connie and I come with you?" Phil asked.

Sam shook her head. "Not a good idea. I'm involved because I couldn't let these ladies die in Otherwhere. They didn't end up there voluntarily. Considering the circumstances, the Grey Ladies may give them and me a pass, but they won't be as gracious with you and Connie."

"But—" Phil started to say.

"No, Phillippa," Ares murmured. "Samantha is correct. She has earned her place through her trials and compassion. I fear for both you and Constanza should you accompany Samantha and her strays."

"Excuse me?" Shan stared at the Olympian.

Anthea leaned closer to Aisha. "I do not understand the insult."

"The asshat is comparing us to dogs," Aisha growled.

"I am confused," Anthea said. "Dogs are lovely creatures."

"A stray dog in our society refers to one that doesn't have a home," Shan snapped. "And the word bitch is an insult for any woman who doesn't do a man's bidding. Put it together."

"Thank you for the clarification." Anthea turned to Ares. "Not even my

Conflict would dare to insult those under Death's protection." She blinked. "Oh. Never mind."

Shan looked at the priestess. "Have you lost your marbles?"

"I do not have any marbles," Anthea said primly. Aisha choked on her soda, but Anthea continued, "But in our religious texts, Conflict was in love with Death, and She spurned Him because She cared for everyone equally. We all end up in Her embrace at the end of our lives, but Conflict selfishly wanted Her for Himself."

Shan watched Ares. From the flush of his neck, Anthea had nailed the problem. "Really? You're jealous because Sam offered to help us?"

He stood abruptly. "I don't need to be insulted by lesser beings." He disappeared, and the air in the room made a *pop* as it rushed in to replace his mass.

After he was gone, Phil and Sam laughed hysterically.

"In other words, he attempted to elicit jealousy from Sam by paying special attention to me in Tiffany's lab," Anthea said wryly.

"Yep." Shan raised her can of soda. "And you deliciously knocked him down. But a word of advice, losing one's marbles is an expression in our worlds. It means a person is insane."

Anthea grinned. "Then I owe Aisha amends for causing her to choke when I accidentally said I didn't have sanity to begin with. However, a great many of my associates would say my lack of sanity is an accurate assessment."

Shan shook her head and chuckled. Too bad Anthea didn't live in her world. She was a lot of fun, and for a religious person, she had an awesome sense of humor. But the reality of the quest Sam proposed sank past her humor.

"How is this going to work?" Shan asked. "I'm human. I don't have any special powers like you guys do."

"You've got a sentient fae sword with you and an enchanted knife, and you know how to use them," Sam said. "None of us are helpless little hobbits."

"Hobbits?" Anthea's eyebrows rose.

"We'll explain it to you later," Aisha said. "But we need to work on your aim with those lightning bolts."

"The lightning strike in Otherwhere was you?" Sam stared at Anthea with new respect in her eyes. "I've got to agree with Aisha on that one." Sam turned to Phil.

"I've got her, but it's going to be a real fast crash course." Phil looked at Anthea. "Feel up to going to an isolated area to practice?"

"How can you teach me?" Anthea cocked her head.

Phil held up her right hand. Static arced between her fingers and down her forearm.

Shan laughed. "Damn right she can teach you!"

"Very well, then." Anthea set aside her can of soda and stood. "I will appreciate any guidance you could offer since I have no one to teach me in my world. Do we need any special dress or equipment?"

"Nope." Phil grinned as she rose and held out her hand. "Come with me."

Anthea clasped Phil's outstretched palm, and the pair disappeared. The pop of displaced air was a little louder this time.

"Don't worry, Shan," Aisha said. "We have your back."

"It's a matter of being humble and honest with the Grey Ladies from what everyone has told me," Sam added.

Shan and Aisha stared at Sam.

"I know I'm a little too honest," Sam admitted.

"It was the humble part that worries us," Aisha said.

Shan laughed again. If the situation wasn't so weird and troubling, she would love to hang out with these ladies for longer.

"Did you learn anything from Phil's dad about these demons who showed up in our respective universes?" Aisha asked.

Sam shook her head. "None of my associates has an indication of what they are. I'm hoping the Grey Ladies might give us a clue so you guys can protect your worlds, and I can keep them out of mine."

"Mind if I ask a question?" Shan asked.

"Sure." Sam reached for another Twinkie.

"I've never heard of a god named Norman. Who is he?"

Sam ripped open the cellophane. "Here in my universe, whoever you call out for at the moment of death is who picks up your soul. Generally, it's the version of Death from your religion. So, if you don't have a religion, Norman gets you."

"What—how does that even work?" Shan asked.

"Well, the souls need to go somewhere. You're an engineer, right? You understand the law of the conservation of energy." Sam shrugged as she took a bite of yellow cake and crème.

Shan leaned against the back of the couch. "I guess I never thought about death that way."

"So, we do have souls?" Aisha asked.

Sam swallowed her bite of Twinkie. "Every living thing has a soul, spirit, or whatever you want to call it. From the lowliest protozoa to the largest space whales—" She stopped abruptly and made a face.

"Telepathy?" Shan whispered.

"I think so," Aisha whispered back.

"Sorry about that." Sam took another bite of her Twinkie. "Miko's raising hell about the pizza delivery, and she's making Leona yell at me. What were we talking about?"

"Protozoa and space whales having souls," Shan prompted.

Sam waved her Twinkie at Aisha. "Don't give me that look, counselor.

Space whales really exist. Point being, everything has to go somewhere when they die. For humans, Norman gets the folks who don't believe in a deity or question any deity's existence."

"And he gets the protozoa and the amoebas and the space whales?" Shan was trying really hard to wrap her mind around what Sam was saying, but this was wilder than Grandmother Wong telling Shan about her real identity.

Sam held up her hand. "No, the amoebas have their own gods. Blobby is actually a pretty cool person for being an asexual mass of goo."

"Blobby?" Aisha seemed to have as much of a problem with these revelations as Shan was.

"That's what I call them." Sam shrugged again. "I can't pronounce their actual name without turning into an amoeba myself. It involves the rate of osmosis."

"Maybe we should pick up some ice cream and go back to Bebe's house," Shan suggested because she really didn't know how much more of this alien world she could handle.

CHAPTER 23

Aisha selected two more slices of pizza from the various take-out boxes on Bebe's kitchen island. She hadn't been this hungry since she was pregnant with Mitch. Shan had already gobbled a couple of slices before she headed back to the room Bebe referred to as the conservatory. Together with Tiffany and Phil's husband Alex, the trio attempted to repair the Ghost Owl suit before their little group of castaways left tomorrow. Straightening Shan's bent knife had been a breeze in comparison. Aisha headed back to the family room with her plate, but she stopped short in the doorway at the sight of her mother-in-law.

Sam stood facing Xquic. However, Bebe, Anthea, and Phil sat frozen on the couch and chairs.

"Xquic? What are you doing here?" For a brief instant, Aisha believed her prayers had been answered, and she had a way home.

But the woman who turned toward Aisha had no recognition in her dark eyes. "You are mine, but not mine." This universe's version of her mother-in-law stepped closer and examined Aisha. "Fascinating."

Behind Xquic, Sam sighed. "I told you so. I may be young and ignorant about a lot of shit compared to the rest of you, but I don't deliberately steal my co-workers' powers or the souls owed to them."

"Steal powers?" Aisha looked from Xquic to Sam and back again.

"Not steal per se." Xquic smiled graciously. "I felt your harmony with one of my sons." She rubbed her abdomen, and only then did Aisha notice the slight bulge under Xquic's Mayan-style dress. "Given the direction the music came from, I feared Samantha had—"

"Had stolen something of yours." Sam rolled her eyes.

"Had made a well-meaning mistake like you did with Baron Samedi's adherent. I apologize to you, Samantha." Xquic didn't bother to look at the younger death goddess, and she winked at Aisha. "Did I have daughters in your universe?"

"No, ma'am." It didn't hurt to add Aunt Queenie's old-fashioned Southern charm. "I'm married to my version of Xbalanque. I developed HRSP while I was pregnant, and my mother-in-law decided to make the condition permanent in order to protect her grandson."

"What is HRSP?" Xquic asked.

"Hormone-related superpowers." Aisha smiled. "It happens to some women during pregnancy when either the father or the baby is a super."

"Interesting. And what is the me of your universe like?" This Xquic peered at her with genuine curiosity.

"Intensely protective of her sons." Aisha chuckled. "I'm thankful she approved of me as a spouse to Xbalanque."

"And is your Hunahpu also wed in your universe?"

Aisha laughed even louder. "He and my friend Qiang will make it official next spring, but they've been living together for the last couple of years."

"Did your me give your friend powers as well?"

"No, ma'am. She had powers long before she met Hunahpu."

"Enjoy your meal, and best wishes on your journey home, child." Xquic leaned close and kissed Aisha's cheek before she teleported out of the house.

"Sam, you and your friends give new meaning to the speed of people coming and going here." Aisha touched the spot where she'd been kissed. Her skin tingled a bit, but not in a bad way.

"Let's hope the good luck charm she just laid on you helps our mission," Sam muttered.

"Is that what she did?" Aisha turned to look at the death goddess.

Sam grinned. "Seems you make friends and influence people no matter what universe you're in, Ms. Franklin-Garcia."

As Aisha sat on the couch next to Anthea with her plate of pizza, she hoped this Xquic's good luck charm didn't backfire on any of her new friends.

CHAPTER 24

Sam did her damnedest to project confidence the next morning over breakfast. Approaching the Grey Ladies wasn't going to be easy, and she'd beg if she had to. The fear she'd felt when Duncan was murdered and his soul was missing had rattled her as fiercely as an eight-point-zero tremblor in the *National Scoop* offices. The feeling right now was at least a six-point-five. She couldn't let these ladies go through the same pain.

Late last night, Tiffany delivered her calculations on everyone's quantum frequencies. Sam hoped the Grey Ladies would know which universes matched the numbers Tiffany had texted. Her sister-in-law added as much as she liked their visitors, she couldn't imagine never seeing her children again.

At least, Aisha and Shan admitted they had significant others. Aisha mentioned her son. Sam smiled to herself at the thought of Shan's pregnancy, but it would be best if she didn't reveal her knowledge to the engineer. Tiffany had been irritated as hell when Sam said she knew Tiffany was pregnant with Ellie from the change in her body odor.

Anthea didn't have the luxury of admitting she was in love with her High Brother Luc. Sam knew Anthea had told the truth to Ares when she said she wasn't allowed to have intimate relations. Sam remembered the pain of being told she couldn't have children. While things had changed for her when she became a full goddess, it wasn't a matter of simply fixing

Anthea. Sam would have to kill the woman and resurrect her as a goddess. Her instinct said Anthea wouldn't appreciate the offer any more than Sam's brother Max had after his death.

This morning, Shan and Aisha had taken over cooking duties. Out of courtesy to Anthea, they made breakfast burritos. The priestess declared them as good as her cook Deborah's back in Orrin.

"So how do we get to wherever the Fates are?" Aisha sat down with her own plate of tortillas, eggs, cheese, and bacon.

"Please tell us we don't have to go back to Otherwhere." Shan shuddered.

"No, not through Otherwhere, but we need to pass through Purgatory," Sam admitted.

Aisha and Shan stared at her.

"What is this Purgatory?" Anthea asked.

Sam's throat closed up, and she couldn't choke out the words. Her own actions resulted in a good friend being sent there permanently as a punishment.

"It depends on which religious teachings you believe," Bebe said. "For some, it's a place where the supreme deity sends you if you haven't done enough good to go to Heaven or enough bad to be sent to Hell. For others, Purgatory is a last chance at redemption."

Anthea frowned. "And you believe you should be rewarded for doing the right thing and punished for doing wrong?"

"I don't personally." Bebe chuckled as she spread cherry preserves on her English muffin. "My people believe everyone ends up in the same place with the Goddess when we die, regardless of their acts on earth."

Anthea shook her head. "I honestly do not understand how you can keep all of your religious concepts straight."

"We don't," Sam said. "We have a lot of wars in our universe due to differences in religious beliefs. So let's not start one here before I can get you guys home."

"I beg your forgiveness." Anthea inclined her head. "I view the matter as an intellectual puzzle. I didn't mean to disparage anyone's beliefs."

"Don't worry about it." Sam took a deep breath and released it. "Let's finish breakfast, suit up, and hit the potty before we head out."

"Potty?" Poor Anthea was once again thoroughly confused.

"Relieve yourself." Sam grinned. "I can't guarantee I can find you a restroom once we leave Los Angeles."

CHAPTER 25

Anthea felt much better inside her own clothing once again. And they were exceptionally clean, with only the vaguest hint of whatever soap Bebe's people had used. Aisha was dressed in her peculiar armor and helm. Shan and Sam's family managed to restore it to full working order.

Shan was the only one not dressed in her original clothing since the demon had dragged her from her home in her sleepwear. Their hosts provided leggings, a white tunic made of knitted cotton, a vest, and sturdy boots. The leggings and vest felt like leather to the touch, but the garments were made of a different material that wasn't their plastic, nor was it ceramic, but an odd blend of both.

Just like Aisha's armor.

Their hosts also provided sheaths for both Shan's sword and knife as well as a harness to carry them with a knapsack attached for her old clothing and canvas shoes.

Sam shifted into her coat, leggings, and boots before she teleported them to the front of another estate. This one looked similar to Bebe's home, but the walls were stone instead of brick, and the gate wasn't made of iron.

"Is this gate made of hepatizon?" Anthea asked.

"Yes, but it's got fae magick running through it, so whatever you do, don't touch it," Sam warned as she pressed a button. In the distance, bells chimed.

"What will it do to us?" Aisha asked.

"Not you. Anthea." Sam gestured at Shan. "Fae magick and witch magick don't play nice when they mix as Shan and Anthea found out in Otherwhere.

Anthea gritted her teeth. That explained the feeling of ants crawling along her skin. Given the shock Shan's sword gave her with an innocent touch, she wasn't about to grab the bars of this strange gate.

"What's hepatizon?" Shan whispered.

"It's an alloy of gold, silver, and copper." Anthea smiled ruefully. "In my world, it's far too soft to be used as real defensive or offensive uses."

Shan giggled. "Not to mention very expensive."

"Truly."

The itchy feeling could equally come from the invisible watchers in the trees behind the wall. She couldn't see them, but the vague, blurry spots among the branches reveal their presence.

A woman approached the gate. Her exposed skin was a peculiar yellow-green. It wasn't the color of an ill human. The odder thing was her hair was the same color as her skin.

"Sam, she isn't human," Anthea murmured.

"No, she's fae," Sam answered. "Everyone chill and stay next to me. Whatever you do, don't make an aggressive move, no matter what any fae does. And they will bait you."

The woman glared at Sam through the bars. This didn't bode well, but Anthea resisted the urge to twitch. Intimidation tactics were the same no matter the type of people who used them.

After a long staring match, the woman signaled to one of the hidden watchers. The gate hummed and swung open without anyone touching it. If only Phil could have taught Anthea how to harness the power of lightning the way these people did. Such a skill would go far to guard a city against demons.

At least, Phil had been able to teach her some self-control. Aisha confirmed her friend Qiang had the same skill with lightning and used it against demons. The Temples' next quest would be to find children with this particular talent as well as those with Light talents in their war against the demons.

Anthea forced her shoulders to relax as she followed Sam through the opening.

"Let me see the witch's face," the fae woman snarled.

Sam stopped just inside the wall, as did the rest of their little group. If the fae thought to close their gate, Sam and Aisha's raw strength would stop it.

Sam let out an exaggerated sigh. "Why, Sapphire?"

"I'm not putting the duke's safety at risk." Sapphire lifted her chin, daring Sam to challenge her.

"It's all right, Sam." Anthea pushed back her hood. Normally, a justice didn't go out in public without wearing her hood. However, her red eyes were sometimes quite useful in gaining the cooperation of others.

Like most humans who were surprised by her unusual eye color, there was a collective gasp from Sapphire and several of her unseen compatriots.

"What in Danu's name did you do to yourself, child?" the fae woman blurted.

"What was necessary to save my people." Anthea watched Sapphire for a long moment before she added, "If you want us off your property, please allow Sam to do what she must. We will all be satisfied to vacate the premises once she is done."

Sapphire pursed her lips, but she said nothing more. She pivoted on obscenely high boot heels and marched up the road.

Neither Sam nor Anthea said anything more. Their little group followed the ill-tempered fae to a large house hidden amongst the trees and bushes.

Anthea stared at the strange structure. The stone forming the base of the building was the only thing normal about it. However, the wood above the stone was still alive. She remained silent though. Any comments or questions may not be taken well.

A man walked out of the front door as they approached. He was barely Shan's height, thin-framed, and dressed in silks. His sly smile reminded her of Crown Prince Po, but his expression had an edge of dislike.

"Darling Samantha, doesn't Constanza wish to play with us anymore?" he said.

"This isn't a normal situation, Your Grace." Sam's stiff posture said she hadn't let go of her anger over the fae queens' orders to assassinate her. "I wouldn't have come here if Morrigan hadn't requested I meet her here."

A bell chimed, similar to the soft silver sound of the small bells that decorated a Love priestess's robes and veil. Anthea looked around, but there was no one else present. And definitely no bells.

"Our Lady is waiting for you in the grove." The duke motioned with a slim finger. "Come."

Once again, silence reigned as they followed this duke away from his manor. A path ran through the woods surrounding the back of the home. Aisha dropped back to pace Sapphire. Anthea release the breath she didn't realize she'd been holding. Good to know she wasn't the only one concerned about their group's safety.

The woods themselves were odd. No morning sun warmth reached the ground, and there was a slight chill in the air. The blurs of the guards leapt from limb to limb, escorting their noble. Anthea felt as if she walked through the shadow of a large building. Or a gigantic cliff.

At the end of the path was a clearing. A woman stood in the center. No, a goddess from the aura around her. However, she didn't glow like Sam had. Dark blue blood stained the simple shift the woman wore.

Unlike the two fae, the woman smiled warmly. "Sam! Such a pleasure to see you." But as she said the words, her pleasant expression fell, and her attention locked on Shan.

"How did that human obtain the Sword of Lugh?" She stalked forward.

Anthea shifted to protect Shan, though mindful of Sam's warning, she kept her hands off her own blades.

Sam stepped in front of the angry goddess. "Morrigan, they aren't from our universe. That's not our Lugh's sword." Sam glanced at Shan. "Plus, she's the granddaughter of Kuan Yin. Do you really want her to respond if you start beating on the kid?"

"I would still know how—"

"Rain, or rather my universe's Morrigan, gave it to my husband Jamal with permission," Shan answered. "My husband is descended from Lugh through Cu Chulainn."

The goddess stopped abruptly. "Let me see the knife."

Anthea stepped to the side. Shan pulled her copper knife from its sheath and held it out to Morrigan hilt first.

The goddess grasped the knife and turned it over in her hands, examining every bit of the weapon. "This is mine, and not mine." She looked at Shan with a rueful smile. "If your Morrigan is anything like me, I'm sure you earned it." She murmured something in Keltic under her breath and handed the knife back to Shan.

"I miss her," Shan said softly as she sheathed her knife.

"Are the crows still watching you?" Morrigan asked.

Shan's eyes widened. "How did you know?"

Morrigan cupped the young woman's cheek. "Trust me, she is keeping you and your family safe. We don't forsake our chosen warriors." She eyed the duke. "No matter how idiotic they may act at times."

Anthea stifled the burble of laughter threatening to erupt from her chest.

Morrigan scowled at her. "You find me amusing, child?"

"Only your choice of words, Lady Morrigan." Anthea smiled. "I have similar feelings for an idiotic prince I'm currently protecting. Or rather, I was protecting him until I accidentally fell into the Otherwhere."

Morrigan glared at the duke. "You could learn much from this one, Millanthropas."

"Yes, m'lady." He lowered his head, but the tension in his lithe body increased.

It was a good thing Sam was taking her home. Anthea didn't like the idea of making more enemies.

"Come with me." Morrigan pivoted and headed into the woods. However, she didn't follow a path. The vegetation simply parted for her to pass without bruising the foliage.

"All right, kids," Sam said. "Hold hands while we cross the street." She grabbed Shan's hand. Anthea took Shan's free hand in her own right. Aisha's gloved palm took Anthea's left.

Their group followed Morrigan into the shadowy woods and into a multi-colored sphere of light.

CHAPTER 26

A wave of dizziness swept over Shan as she stepped through the fae portal, but it wasn't as bad as jumping into and out of Otherwhere. If it weren't for Sam holding her upright though, she would have dropped to her knees. Her breakfast burritos threatened to make a comeback as it was.

"Slow, deep breaths, Shan," Sam murmured in her ear.

She closed her eyes and did as the goddess suggested. The nausea receded.

"This place is so beautiful," Aisha said.

Shan opened her eyes. Purple afterimages still floated in her vision, but they didn't diminish the marvelous sight. White birches arced skyward, their tops aflame with orange leaves. Songbirds she didn't recognize flitted from branch to branch.

However, their music stopped abruptly when a flock of crows dropped from the crystal blue sky. One of the crows lit on Morrigan's left shoulder. The goddess no longer wore a bloody white shift. Instead, she wore a leather dress with matching boots that were the same maroon as her hair. A battle ax dangled from her black leather belt. Everything was trimmed with gold Keltic geometric designs.

"Can you continue, Mistress Shan?" Morrigan asked.

"Yes, ma'am." She smiled weakly and pulled a foil package from the front pocket of her new pants. "Brought Dramamine with me since I didn't know how many teleportations and portals I'd be dealing with." She popped one of the ginger chews into her mouth.

"Don't take too many of those," Sam warned. "I don't want you passing out on us."

Anthea leaned close to Shan and murmured, "May I have one of those? I don't want to waste the excellent burritos you and Aisha made this morning."

Shan pushed one of the chews through its protective foil and into Anthea's waiting palm before she shoved the package back into her pants pocket.

The fae goddess led them through the birches. The crows formed an escort around them. The birds alternated between flying and walking.

"Do you mind if I ask some questions while we walk, Lady Morrigan?" Shan asked.

"The answer will depend on the question."

Shan swallowed her old grief. The woman sounded so much like her Rain. And Morrigan's comment was the same reply when Shan had asked the same questions.

"My grandmother's neighbor said the fae lands were divided between the Summer and Winter Courts. Why is it autumn here?"

"To use Samantha's vernacular, this is the Neutral Zone." Morrigan flashed a grin at the other goddess. "The Courts come here to parley. From midsummer to midwinter, this is how the Neutral Zone appears."

"So, from midwinter to midsummer, the Neutral Zone resembles spring?

"Yes."

A zillion questions Shan had never had the chance to ask Rain spilled from her as they walked. Occasionally, Anthea asked about some quirks between their respective styles of magick. Aisha and Sam seemed content to listen while they walked. On some particular points, Lexi hummed in agreement. On a couple of points, the sword squealed an objection.

Morrigan took everything in stride. She patiently debated the cardinal points and their corresponding elements and colors with the sentient sword.

All too soon, the birches' bark no longer glowed a brilliant white, and their leaves dulled to brown where they still clung to their branches. Some kind of creatures shuffled beneath the detritus on the ground.

Shan knew better than to ask what crawled beneath the dead leaves in the fae lands. Recognizing an entity focused its attention on you. Not necessarily in a healthy way.

A shriek came from behind her. Aisha's vocal modulator couldn't totally compensate for the second girly scream. Shan stopped and turned to find Aisha hovering a yard above the forest floor.

"What the hell just crawled over my boot?"

"Aisha, look at me." Shan couldn't be sure the superhero complied with her polarized visor covering her face. "I need you listen. Really listen. Nothing was on your foot. But we are going be in big trouble if you keep shrieking like that."

"B-b-but—" From the motion of her head, Aisha was trying to examine the ground with her suit's equipment.

Sam levitated to reach Aisha, pushed up her visor, and cupped her helmet in both hands. "Listen to the kid, Ghost Owl. Some of the things here like to play tricks, and they're willing to risk Morrigan's wrath to do so. You lose it here, and I can't help you. You're a lawyer. If a term ain't in the contract, it's not enforceable. Do you understand?"

Aisha gulped a couple of times before she forced herself to exhale. "Five by five, boss lady."

Sam nodded before she slowly descended back to the leaf-covered ground, pulling Aisha along with her.

Shan breathed a sigh of relief when something grabbed her by her right ankle and jerked her off her feet. It dragged her through dead leaves and branches. Their crow escort didn't so much as squawk at the disturbance.

"Not again," Shan muttered.

CHAPTER 27

Aisha launched herself toward Shan. The engineer had her copper knife out, but at the rate the root bumped her around on the ground, she couldn't turn herself around to reach the tendril wrapped around her ankle, dragging her to God knew where.

After landing two yards from Shan's ankles, Aisha dug in her heels, seized what appeared to be a root wrapped around Shan's boot, and pulled. The thing holding the younger woman was as strong as Aisha.

"Don't use steel!" Sam warned.

Aisha looked over her shoulder. The two goddesses still stood where she had her little freak-out. And the root was slowly dragging her and Shan to its final destination.

Anthea raced toward Shan with her sword drawn. At Sam's warning, Anthea muttered something in her own language. She slid to a stop beside Shan.

"Would Lexi allow me to use her?" Anthea said between her panting.

The sword pealed, and Aisha would've sworn the dang thing said yes in English.

Anthea drew Lexi, but she didn't hack at the root. No, she laid the blade against it.

Lexi crooned a strange melody. The root stopped dragging Aisha and Shan. It slowly unwound itself from Shan's leg.

"Anthea, leave Lexi and get Shan back to Sam," Aisha dropped the section of root she held.

"I can't leave her behind," Shan protested.

"We won't, but the minute Lexi releases the root from her spell, it'll be on you again." Aisha held out her gloved hand and pulled Shan to her feet. "Climb on top of Sam if you have to. I'll grab Lexi and fly her back to you." When Shan didn't answer, Aisha added sharply, "You feel me, girl?"

Either her tone or her words shook Shan out of indecision. The younger woman nodded sharply and ran for Sam.

Aisha crouched next to Anthea and laid her own palm in the blade. Lexi continued to hum her song.

"Normally, I would freeze the time around the tentacle until we all retreated from its reach," the priestess murmured.

"Tentacle?" Aisha whispered.

"There's an illusion on it." Anthea snorted. "I apologize, but if I tried a revelation spell in this fae land—"

"Thank you for not blowing us to smithereens." Aisha grinned. It was reassuring to know she hadn't imagined the thing that brushed over her boot.

The priestess didn't bother with a blessing or anything like that. She rose and ran after Shan.

Aisha waited until both women reached Sam before she shifted to hold Lexi by the hilt. If this sword had half the powers the various stories said it did, she didn't want to accidentally slice her own hand off.

"Okay, Lexi, we're going on three, two, one." Aisha shot skyward with the sword in her hand.

Beneath her, a roar filled the woods. Something shook the twisted birch trees, sending a flurry of dead leaves into the air.

Something out of a nightmare crawled toward the people. It no longer wore the illusion of being a tree root. The thing was as big as an elephant, but covered with scales instead of hide. It had eight solidly black eyes. Flailing tentacles sought the potential prey on the ground.

Or they did until Morrigan stepped between their party of castaways and the monster.

"Cease," she commanded.

The creature whined and moaned. Its tentacles quivered.

Aisha landed next to Shan and handed Lexi to her. Shan didn't bother sheathing her sword, and Anthea had drawn hers. Aisha charged her wrist tasers.

"Are you questioning my command?" Morrigan narrowed her eyes. A few of the crows fluttered between their mistress and the creature, cawing their support for their queen.

A low bass note came from the creature.

"You had your chance." Morrigan shrugged. "You failed. Begone."

The creature snuffled and whimpered as it slunk back through the dark, gnarled trees.

Aisha frowned as the incident replayed through her mind. Neither Sam nor Morrigan had lifted a finger when that creature first grabbed Shan. Anthea and Aisha had gotten lucky. The thread of memory turned into a tangled skein of suspicion.

What the hell was she going to do if Sam wasn't taking them to the Fates like she promised?

CHAPTER 28

Sam would have bitten through her tongue if it weren't for her nanites repairing the flesh. She hated these stupid games testing a mortal's mettle. Even worse, she couldn't say a damn thing without invalidating the challenges the three women faced. From the burning broccoli odor seeping from Aisha's Ghost Owl suit, she was more than a little suspicious of Sam's integrity.

And that sucked. Sam liked these ladies. They were the kind of people she would have hung out with when she was still human.

If she had actual girlfriends way back then.

But her little group of castaways had passed their first test with flying colors. So maybe, just maybe, they would survive to reach their homes.

Stupid god rules.

The deformed trees arced their branches overhead to form a sort of tunnel in the gloom as Morrigan led them to the exit from the fae lands. No other entities bothered the group of women and crows.

Dirt and debris gathered around the trunks of the warped birches, growing higher. The crow stopped flying their circular escort. Instead, the majority hopped and walked. One flew point, and another crow acted as their rearguard.

The dirt changed to clay and rose over their heads. Still her three wayward ladies said nothing. They didn't question aloud what happened with

Morrigan's beast. And they were all way too smart not to notice Sam hadn't done a damn thing like she had in Otherwhere.

This mess had all the potential to blow up in her face. This wasn't like Tiffany getting pissed at her. These three ladies had real power at their fingertips.

Actually, Tiffany being pissed at her would result in her sister-in-law building a weapon capable of taking out any god. Tiffany had all the makings of a mad scientist or a supervillain. What if the version of Tiffany in Aisha's universe *was* a supervillain?

"Penny for your thoughts."

Sam jumped at Aisha's words. "What? Why?"

"You've been rather quiet."

"Actually, I'm scared my sister-in-law is a supervillain in your world."

"Tiffany?" Aisha frowned. She'd left her visor up since her encounter with Morrigan's beast. Yep, smart. She realized the electronics in her suit couldn't be trusted in the fae lands. "She seems to have her act together."

Sam decided to ignore the not-so-subtle dig that she did not have her own shit together.

Before she could formulate a reply, Aisha asked, "If she's married to Ptolemy in Jake's body, how is she your sister-in-law?"

"Tiffany's first husband is—was my brother Max." The old grief tugged at the scars on her heart. She'd lost too many people she loved in the course of becoming a deity and saving her world from an ancient dinosaur god who wanted to reclaim Earth. "Her eldest daughter is my niece."

"I take it she started seeing Ptolemy after she was widowed?" Aisha said.

"Actually, she started dating Jake." Sam checked Shan, but she was thoroughly involved in a conversation with Morrigan. "I think she did it because I was engaged to Jake long before I married her uncle Duncan. Except I wanted to see them both happy. Jake planned to propose, but he died in the accident on set—"

"And that's when Ptolemy decided to possess Jake's body," Aisha finished.

"The idiots involved in that mess needed both Jake and Ptolemy's permission for the soul swap." Sam shook her head. "Dead people make stupid decisions. Including me."

"Mm-hmmm." But that was all Aisha said.

Damn, what would be worse? Getting stabbed with two magic swords that could explode her innards all over the landscape or have the crap beat out of her by a real super-strong superhero?

Sam chewed on her tongue some more. She needed to figure out a way to earn the lost women's trust back, or she just may find out the limits of her own godhood.

CHAPTER 29

Anthea breathed a little prayer of relief when they reached the doorway to which Morrigan led them. The path had turned to a full tunnel beneath the earth. She could feel the weight of the soil and rock over and around them.

And the enclosed space triggered her claustrophobia.

She ran through a number of High Sister Mya's methods for easing her growing panic. Those tricks did nothing to stop the sweat dampening her armpits or trickling down her back.

Morrigan rested her left hand on the lever of the bronze door in the stone wall. "This leads to the dream lands. Sam, you first. You should sense the door to Purgatory from here."

Sam nodded and stepped forward.

It had taken every ounce of will for Anthea not to run the goddess through with her sword. Did this version of Death think Anthea hadn't noticed she'd done nothing to defend them from Morrigan's creature?

Well, technically, Sam had offered a hint. Like Anthea hadn't remembered what happened with her sword and Shan's when they stabbed the demon at the same time in Otherwhere, but still a hint.

The oldest religious texts from before Balance's Revelation said the Twelve could not act directly for one human's benefit. However, they often offered advice and tools if the protagonist of the tale displayed the proper respect and humility before the Twelve.

Was that the problem? Sam, as an avatar of Death, couldn't directly assist them, but only offer them advice on this journey?

Anthea cursed at herself. With all the assassination attempts over the last two years, she distrusted everyone and everything, and her pride and suspicion may get her companions killed.

However, neither goddess glanced at her. Morrigan opened the door. Fresh air flowed into the tunnel. It was all Anthea could do not to race through the exit herself.

Sam stepped into the sand and tilted her head like a canine searching for a scent. Finally, she said, "Got it."

"Go n-éirí an bóthar libh!" Morrigan stepped back and nodded to Anthea and her companions.

The three of travelers stepped through the doorway. A metallic creak came from behind them. Anthea looked over her shoulder, but the doorway and the tunnel were gone.

Sand surrounded them, endless sand to the deep blue horizon. But this was normal looking sand. The grains whispered as the slight breeze pushed the top layer end-over-end. It reminded her of the descriptions of the Great Desert of the Cradle. Few could survive its heat unprepared.

She looked up at the sky overhead, as did Aisha. But there was no sun or moon to indicate the time of day of this place.

"I don't recognize any of the constellations," Aisha commented.

"None of the stars look familiar either." Shan looked at Sam. "Where are we?"

"We're not in Kansas anymore." Sam waved. "Come on. We need to get to the way station before daybreak."

"Daybreak?" Shan looked around them before she looked at the odd device strapped to her wrist that Sam's friends had supplied her. "It's only ten a.m."

"It's ten a.m. in my California." Sam said. "Not here. And stay close. The critters here won't turn down the opportunity to eat human if you give them half a chance."

Sam took the lead, and they followed her.

"Aisha," Anthea whispered. "Put your visor back in place. We want as much warning as we can get."

"Thinking the same thing, girlfriend." The superhero pushed the face shield back over her visage.

Anthea lost track of her bootsteps as they traversed the desert. She occasionally heard cries and growls in the distance. Hopefully, the sounds meant the predators of this land were finding easier prey than the four travelers.

However, her stomach began its own growling.

Shan laughed. "I agree with Anthea. Can we please take a small break, Sam? We aren't superhuman like you and Aisha."

"A small one." However, Sam still looked tense. Like she expected something to happen at any moment.

Was this another hint? Would something jump out at them in this wasteland?

Of course, it would.

It was only a question of when.

CHAPTER 30

Shan dug the granola bars out of her pack and passed them out to the other women. Sam declined the granola bar, but she pulled a Twinkie out of her coat pocket. There had to be some correlation between her being a death goddess and her obsession with the yellow sponge cakes. But Shan wasn't comfortable asking.

Which was weird because she had no problem chattering away with Morrigan.

According to Shan's watch, they'd been trudging through this desert for the last five hours. The stars cast enough light to see her companions. The breeze was cool enough she wasn't soaked in sweat, but when she sat down, her calves reminded her she hadn't been hiking since her honeymoon. Running a couple of miles on pavement every morning wasn't the same as trudging through sand. The other three women dropped on the sand so they formed a circle. Funny how some of the safety measures Mom taught her while living in New York City worked in a forest or a desert wilderness.

"These are tastier than hard tack and dried meat during a long journey," Anthea mumbled around a mouthful of her sticky bar. "What is the sweetner? It doesn't taste like honey or maple syrup."

"Corn syrup," Aisha stated.

"And we don't recommend taking that idea back to your world," Sam said.

"Why not?" Anthea frowned.

"It can do some weird things to your metabolism, and it can be addictive." Shan held up her bar. "Are you losing your bees, too, Sam?"

"Unfortunately." Sam grimaced. "Ironically, by totally destroying Mount Rainier ten years ago, I may have resurrected the bugs."

Aisha snickered.

"What's so funny?" Sam demanded.

"The idea of zombie bees buzzing all over the place." Aisha laughed some more.

"That's not funny." Sam glared at the superhero. "It would be a hell of a lot worse than zombie mosquitos attacking you. Which actually happened to me."

"What happens when a mosquito bites a god?" Shan licked her fingers.

"In my case, the live ones explode." Sam shook her head. "The zombie ones resurrect into live ones."

"But if the zombie ones who resurrected bite you again?" Shan couldn't stop her questions.

Sam grimaced. "They explode."

"Shan, I believe the point of her story is do not bite Sam," Anthea said.

All four of them broke up laughing.

The goddess rose to her feet. "If you've had enough of a rest, we really need to continue."

Shan took a sip of water from her canteen before she slipped it back in her pack. Despite sharing it with Anthea and Aisha, the amount hadn't seemed to have diminished during their trek through the fae forest or across this desert. Was Sam keeping it filled somehow?

If she was, Shan knew she couldn't ask. According to Grandmother Wong's lessons, to question a deity about their aid meant that aid might be withdrawn. And Shan sure wasn't going to make Anthea and Aisha pay for her curiosity.

After another three hours passed, Shan thought her exhaustion had affected her vision when the stars to her right disappeared and popped back into sight. She paused and stared in that direction.

"Hey, did any of you notice—"

Sam seized Shan's arm and dragged her flat on the sand at the same time Aisha shouted, "Get down!"

She and Anthea threw their bodies to the sand. Something whistled past Shan's right ear, but the scariest part was the silence of the creatures flying over them. She reached for Lexi.

"No!" Sam grabbed Shan's arm. "No blades. Blood will bring more of them."

Aisha launched herself into the air. The stars disappearing and reappearing were the only way Shan could mark Aisha and their foes. The superhero soared and dove while she attempted to distract the birds of prey from the others.

"What kind of birds are those?" Shan yelled.

"Those monsters barely had enough feathers to qualify as birds!" Anthea shouted back.

Unfortunately, their noise attracted the things back to them despite Aisha's best efforts. Except one of the travelers had her own version of anti-aircraft guns and radar.

"Light 'em up, Anthea!" Shan barked.

"What?"

"She means you can see them so blast the bastards with lightning!" Sam yelled.

Shan crossed her fingers her plan would work.

And Anthea wouldn't accidentally electrocute the rest of their party in the process.

CHAPTER 31

Anthea swallowed hard. Hopefully, Phil's lessons hadn't been shaken from her brain. The goddess had taken her to a deserted island in the middle of their Peaceful Sea. They'd practiced until Anthea nearly dropped from exhaustion. But she had known she may never have an opportunity to learn from someone with the same odd abilities as hers again.

Thankfully, the orange bird-like monsters stood out against the dark blue sky to her. The dark green fringe of feathers along their wings and tails didn't hide the beasts' size. And their lighter green beaks and talons were much more worrisome. Aisha couldn't keep them distracted forever. Her maneuverability was the only reason she was still in the air.

Anthea concentrated. Controlled the power arcing between her fingers and snapping along her arms. And took aim.

The bird monster she hit ignited with bright pink fire and plummeted to the sand. Two more of their assailants quickly followed.

One tried to fly away, but Aisha taunted it until it followed her back to Anthea. Aisha darted past, and Anthea launched a fourth lightning bolt. The bird crashed into the top of a nearby dune and slid down the sand until its burning carcass halted a couple of yards from her boots.

The fifth one dove for her. There was no cover, and Sam said not to use a blade. Anthea readied her wards.

Aisha grabbed the last bird from behind before it reached Anthea and wrenched its head. An audible crack drowned out Anthea's gasps. Aisha dropped the last corpse on top of one of the burning ones. The feathers immediately sprouted pink fire. Sam and Shan stood and brushed sand from their clothes.

Aisha landed lightly beside Anthea. "We need to go before the fire attracts unwanted attention. You okay to continue, girl?"

Anthea nodded. "We have to."

"I was going to offer a piggy-back ride." Aisha's humor came through the device that altered her voice.

"Riding a pig is a good way to be trampled in the mud," Anthea replied dryly.

"She meant she'd carry you," Shan said.

"I know what she meant." Anthea smiled. "I stand by my statement." She started walking in the direction Sam had been heading.

Once again, Anthea couldn't help noticing Sam did not raise a finger to help them. Nor would the Twelve be able to answer her prayers. But Anthea couldn't help wishing there was an easier way to get home.

CHAPTER 32

Once Shan's adrenaline burned off from the bird monster attack, the leg cramps set in like a mother, and finally one sent her sprawling on the shifting sand. Without a word, Anthea knelt beside Shan and kneaded the knots in her calves.

"Let me carry you," Aisha said.

"No." More gently, Shan added, "I can do this."

"I hope you can." Sam wore a worried expression while she looked behind them. "False dawn has started."

Shan looked over her shoulder. Sure enough, a pale line of purple highlighted the difference between the sand and sky. She turned back to Sam. "How much longer do we have before sunrise in this place?"

"A candlemark in Anthea's parlance," Sam answered. "And a couple of miles to cover."

Despite Shan's nerves, nothing more dive-bombed their group from the sky. Or burst from the sands to devour them. Heroes always had three tasks to accomplish in a majority of folktales. They shouldn't have anymore challenges until they reached Purgatory.

She hoped.

She tried not to look at her watch as the women alternately walked and

141

jogged the last miles. Behind her, the sky was brightening enough she could tell the difference in the gray and brown of Aisha's Ghost Owl suit.

The light behind them reflected on something in the distance.

"Not much further," Sam said with a hint of relief in her voice.

Shan frowned as they approached what appeared to be a white door and frame standing in the vast expanse of sand. No support. No other structure anywhere nearby. The door looked like any pre-hung door available at any home improvement superstore. However, the doorknob resembled Victorian-era cut glass.

"Finally," Sam drawled as they approach the lonely door.

"This is our destination?" Anthea asked in disbelief.

"Nope. This is Purgatory." Sam twisted the knob and pushed open the door. "The next to last stop." She stepped through the doorframe.

Shan followed and then blinked. She half-expected more sand, but this place resembled a physician's waiting room. A very white waiting room.

Two vinyl couches, one on the left and one straight ahead. A desk. The overhead fluorescent lights. Everything was white except the police officer in his late twenties sitting at the desk and a newspaper folded neatly on the desktop.

"Shan," Anthea hissed.

She stepped to the side so Anthea and Aisha could enter the odd room.

The cop rose and circled the desk so he could embrace Sam. She returned his hug.

"Good to see you, kid," he murmured.

"I'm sorry I can't come more often." She sniffed, and tears swam in the blonde's eyes.

They parted, and Sam wiped away the damp trails on her cheeks before she turned to the trio.

"Guys, this is Fred Ngyuen. He save my ass when I was twelve." Sam gestured at the three ladies with her. "That's Shan, Anthea, and Aisha."

"Shan Wong-Washington?" When she nodded, he snapped his fingers. "I have something for you." He strode behind his desk and pulled open a drawer. He picked up a multicolored cube and handed it to Shan.

"A Rubick's cube?" She frowned at the toy, then at Sam's friend Fred. "Are you asking me to solve it?"

He grimaced. "Not me. The Grey Ladies have a warped sense of humor. And I cannot permit you to go further until you solve it."

"What happens if me or Anthea try solving the cube?" Aisha asked.

Sam sighed. "Anthea can't because she can't see the colors of the stickers. Besides, you've both already had your tests. This is the last one."

Shan's shoulders relaxed. "Easy peasy, lemon squeezy." She accepted the toy and walked over to one of the couches. After removing her pack and flopping onto the vinyl, she started twisting the sides of the cube.

Two hours later, she still hadn't finished the puzzle.

Which didn't make sense. She'd figured out the toy when she was in grade school. Heck, Jamal and she timed each other on how fast they could solve it.

"Think outside the box, Shan," Sam murmured from where she perched on the corner of Fred's desk.

He swatted her arm with his newspaper. "No cheating, young lady."

"You're dead, and I'm a goddess," she shot back. "You can't call me a young lady."

"I was still born before you," he retorted.

Stickers. Outside the box. Sam wasn't trying to screw them over. She had been helping them from the start.

And someone had fucked with the damn stickers.

Shan tried to slide her right index fingernail beneath a blue vinyl sticker and only succeeded in breaking off her nail down to the quick. She grunted at the pain and stuck her injured finger in her mouth.

"Sam's Morrigan blessed your copper knife," Anthea murmured.

Fred didn't object to the priestess making a suggestion.

Shan pulled her knife from its new sheath. The copper tip slid beneath the sticker smoother than room-temperature butter. She quickly rearranged the stickers.

"How does cheating help?" Aisha said, but a bell chimed three times.

"Because these Grey Ladies cheated to set me up," Shan snapped. "If I continued playing by the normal rules, we would have been stuck in this room forever."

A door appeared behind Sam's right shoulder as she jumped off the desk. "Our audience has been granted." She strode to the new door and opened it.

"What's with all the annoying games?" Aisha's voice quivered with anger.

"It's the stupid god rules." Sam shrugged. "I hate them, too, but I can't just grant your wishes. If Norman were here, he blab on and on about Spider-man, power, and responsibility. Blah, blah, blah."

"Let's talk to the Grey Ladies," Anthea said. "I don't know about the rest of you, but I'm ready to go home."

Shan rose and offered the toy back to Fred. He smiled and held up a hand to refuse it. "Return it to them." He inclined his head toward the second door.

Shan nodded. "Thanks, Officer Ngyuen." She strode to the new door and followed the other three through the exit.

She stepped into a Victorian parlor, styled with mahogany wainscoting, cabbage rose wallpaper, and Persian rug in matching colors. An elderly white woman sat across the room. Her white hair was piled artfully on her head, and she wore a burgundy dress with black lace of the same era as the room.

A middle-aged Asian woman sat to Shan's right. Threads of silver graced her temples, but the rest of her hair was black as midnight. She wore a twenty-first century black business suit with a white shawl-collared blouse and sensible black heels.

A Black girl sat to Shan's left, appearing to be around eight. Her hair was braided into pigtails. She wore a blue and white plaid jumper over a white shirt with a Peter Pan collar. Lace-edged socks and Mary Janes covered her feet. She swung her legs impatiently since she couldn't reach the floor from the edge of her chair.

Behind each of the strange females, an ornate mirror hung on the wall. Or rather they looked like mirrors, but nothing was reflected.

"About time you three showed up," the girl snapped.

CHAPTER 33

Aisha wasn't sure what to make of the trio in front of her. She shoved up her visor so they could see her face. "We're sorry for bothering you, ladies, but we need your assistance."

"To get home." The white woman flicked her hand dismissively.

"Did any of you try clicking your heels three times?" the Asian woman mocked.

"Stop making fun of them," the little girl said angrily. "This is a major problem that we need to fix."

"Everything's a major problem to you," the middle-aged woman retorted.

"She's right," the elderly woman stated. "Those damn things are trying to invade the surrounding timelines."

Surprisingly, Sam pushed between Aisha and Shan and curtsied. "I will pay whatever price you demand, ladies. But these three need to go back to their home worlds."

The elderly woman snorted. "We know that. And quit muddying the waters, Samantha. They already earned their passage."

"Sam's right about stupid rules," the little girl argued.

"Broken rules are why the Noktiti are spreading," the middle-aged woman pointed out.

"Noktiti?" Aisha asked. "Is that what Anthea's demons are called?"

"Please, my ladies, tell me how to defeat them," Anthea begged.

The middle-aged woman sighed. "Debts must be paid. We cannot simply grant wishes. We're not djinn."

"I'll pay whatever your—"

Sam slapped her hand over Anthea's mouth before she could finish her sentence. "Shut up, girl. I'm trying to get you home, not enslaved."

"We don't enslaved people," the elderly white woman snapped. However, the little girl rolled her eyes.

"Look, you ladies are obviously concerned about these Noktiti, too." Aisha stepped forward. "They've invaded my world, and from Shan and Anthea's descriptions, they are trying to control Shan's mother-in-law and use her to invade Shan's world. We're not asking for you to fix our problems." Aisha held out her hands. "We just need to know how to stop them."

"You won't need to know, my dear." The elderly white woman smiled. "Once we send all of you back, the timelines will correct themselves."

The mirrors behind each of the Fates rippled and shifted until a picture appeared. Behind the Asian woman, Aisha recognized the picnic table underneath the pin oak tree in Allen George Memorial Park where she and Qiang often met for lunch.

"That's Morrigan's Cauldron," Shan exclaimed as she stared at the mirror behind the little girl.

"The Crimson Palace Square in Naha," Anthea murmured. "But it's empty."

"Forgive us, Chief Justice," the elderly woman said. "We have chosen a time where you can step through without immediately being killed. It does us no good for you to die after we've gone to the trouble of returning you. When you step through, it will be a few hours after your battle."

"For Shan, it will be a few minutes after she was abducted," the little girl stated.

"For Aisha, it will be after Sparx stopped throwing lightning bolts." The middle-aged woman chuckled. "No sense in you getting fried by one of your friends."

Aisha turned to Sam. "I'm really sorry for thinking you were jacking us around."

"Don't sweat it." Sam waved dismissively. "I'd be suspicious of me, too, if I were in your shoes." She grinned. "Or rather your superhero boots."

Aisha laughed and threw her arms around the goddess. "Thanks for your help."

Anthea and Shan each hugged Sam as well and thanked her.

Aisha turned back to the Fates. "What do we do?"

"Just step through," the elderly woman said.

"What about the demons?" Anthea demanded. "If they are invading more worlds than mine—"

The little girl rolled her eyes. "They won't be if you get your ass back to your world."

Aisha approached the mirror showing the Canyon Pointe park.

"Aisha?"

She turned. Shan and Anthea stood behind her. Both women threw their arms around Aisha, and she returned their hugs.

"Nice knowing, you guys," she said.

"Good luck," Shan said before she approached the mirror showing her mother-in-law's store.

"May the Twelve watch over you both," Anthea murmured.

"And you," Aisha said.

Once they were in front of the mirrors showing their respective worlds, Aisha sucked in a deep breath. "On three, ladies. One, two, three."

She stepped forward.

CHAPTER 34

Once her three wayward sisters stepped through their respective portals, Sam glared at the Fates. "Did you tell Anthea the truth? Or do I need to worry about these asshole demons of hers showing up in our world?"

"In your world," the elderly lady corrected. "And no. Once Anthea was returned, her timeline will continue as it should."

"Would you like a ride home, Sam?" the little girl snapped her fingers. The mirror behind her now showed Sam's own living room.

"But I have so many questions," Sam protested.

"We do not answer to you, Samantha," the Victorian Chick chided. "You have your domain, and we have ours."

"Interfering in each others' responsibilities gets all of us in trouble," the little girl said. "Or didn't you learn a darn thing after you butted heads with Baron Samedi?"

"That was—" Sam started.

"A major-ass screw-up." The middle-aged woman rolled her eyes. "But you learned from the experience. So don't do it a second time."

Sam sucked in a deep breath. In saving her husband from a necromancer sworn to Baron Samedi, she lost her brother. The Fates were right. There was a price for everything.

"Is there any way I can see Anthea, Shan, and Aisha again?" she said in a small voice. "They are nice people."

"Even if they were highly suspicious of your motives," the elderly woman teased.

"They had every right to be suspicious," Sam replied. "I couldn't tell them the truth about their tests."

The little girl crossed her arms. "The stupid-ass rules exist for a reason. You think you're doing them favors by giving them the cheat codes. This is life, Sam. Not Grand Theft Auto. Not even we can start the game over because we don't like the results."

"I'm . . . sorry." Sam bowed her head. "I'm still getting used to not being human."

"Deep down, you'll always be human, Sam." The middle-aged woman smiled. This time, it was a genuine one. "That's not necessarily a bad thing."

"Even if I keep my game playing to poker or bridge with my friends?" Sam asked wryly.

"Maybe you should invite us to your game night," the middle-aged woman said.

Sam cocked her head. "Wouldn't that scare the piss out of the other gods?"

"Of course, it would." The Victorian Chick chuckled.

"Or we could play Go Fish or Rummy once in a while," the little girl suggested.

"And maybe some of our suggestions would help improve your game," the middle-aged woman said.

"I would be delighted if you ladies would join us next Saturday night for cards and snacks." Sam curtsied once again.

"And we would be delighted to accept." The middle-aged woman nodded in return.

Sam grinned. This Saturday's poker night would be interesting.

CHAPTER 35

Balance magic tingled across Anthea's skin. A time freeze spell. She whirled around.

Shan and Aisha had started to step through their portals, but their bodies were frozen before they could actually pass through the neat holes in space and time.

Sam stood in front of the Grey Ladies, looking a little lost. Her mouth was partly open as if she had started to say something.

And the Grey Ladies no longer looked quite so human when they rose from their chairs and faced Anthea. All three of them glowed slightly with a purple-ish nimbus, but they no longer wore their strange clothing.

The Lady in the middle wore the accoutrements of Balance Herself. The Lady who had presented herself as a child wore robes with the insignia of Death. And the third Lady wore the tunic and skirt of Mother and carried a traditional grinding stone in her hand.

The last time Anthea faced Balance, panic hadn't let her think. This time, the logic didn't knot her thoughts together.

"Why did You freeze the others?" Anthea asked.

"In order to speak to you privately, for you are Mine." Balance stepped forward. "If you stop the demons in your timeline, they will be stopped for good. They will not have the opportunity to invade Shan's or Aisha's worlds." She chuckled. "Or even Samantha's."

"Because it never happened?"

Balance nodded. "In a sense. The demons already in their worlds will be defeated by them, and the grimoires destroyed. But the demons and their human pets will not be able to summon reinforcements because there are none to call."

That made sense since the other three women existed six centuries in the future. Anthea clasped her hands behind her back, trying to appear as inoffensive as possible. "I don't understand why they cannot know this. It would go to reassure—"

"Because they're all human, my daughter." Balance gestured at the other two portals. "They have freedom of choice. With foreknowledge, they could change the pattern of life as it is meant to be. And even with their good intentions, they could travel to your time and disrupt your tasks."

"But Sam is an aspect of Death," Anthea protested. "She's a part of you."

"But with a human's urges and needs," Death said gently. "At least for now. You don't know how hard it was for her to not interfere in your trials."

"That's why Morrigan accompanied us for the first leg of our journey, isn't it?" Anthea was beginning to understand Sam's annoyance with the "stupid god rules" as she put it.

"Part of the reason, yes," Balance admitted.

"Can I tell my fellow clergy about this discussion?"

Mother sighed. "You can, but don't be surprised if they don't believe you, my dear.

Anthea stared at the wool rug beneath her boots. She couldn't see if the rug had a pattern or if it were a solid color. And for the first time, she truly understood what it was to be a normal human. To face life as the great unknown.

"I understand why you can't tell me what to do to stop the demons." She looked up at the Grey Ladies. "It doesn't mean I have to like it."

"We don't expect you to like it, Anthea," Death murmured. "We did as

Sam finally learned to do. We can give you hints, but you have to listen to them.”

“Or you find me a teacher, so I don’t accidentally kill myself or another human.” Anthea chuckled.

“And so you can find and teach others your skills,” Balance added.

Anthea inclined her head. “Thank you for your wisdom, my Ladies. Perhaps you should resume your seats so I can go home and get on with my mission.”

Their clothing rustled, the time freeze spell ended, and Anthea stepped through the window to her world—

—and inhaled the damp, salty air of a seaside city. It was incredibly quiet around the square in front of the Crimson Palace. Crickets sang, and early spring flowers filled the cool air with a variety of scents. Neither the sun nor moon glowed dully above her head.

In contrast, blood stained the stones and pavers of the street leading into the gates of the palace. No conventional lanterns shone. No yellow and orange faces of guards peeked over the walls of the palace either. The only hint of magic lay to the south of the palace.

In Naha’s Temple District.

The Grey Ladies said they were sending her back to Naha a few hours after the clash between the Ryukyuan forces and the demon army. With a start, Anthea realized the Grey Ladies hadn’t said who won.

She sucked in a deep breath and released it. If the Temple of Death had to release their last resort spells, she wouldn’t be alive for the questions to gather in her mind. The best place to start looking for answers would be at the city’s Temple of Balance. She turned south and followed the scent of cherry blossoms along the city’s main avenue.

CHAPTER 36

Shan stopped at her second step. The antique light fixtures still glowed overhead. The musty smell of used books mixed with the odor of the herbs, incense, and candles the shop carried. The demon grimoire still sat open on the cashwrap counter. Items had been knocked over when she'd fought the demon, but nothing seemed to be broken. The red neon sign at her grandparents' restaurant across the street blinked steadily through the front window.

And her in-laws Phylicia and Dante peered at her through the front door window.

Shan rushed over to unlock the gates and push them open while Phylicia unlocked the door itself. The bells on the door rang cheerful notes as the door burst open.

"What in the Goddess's many names is going on over here?" Phylicia stalked into her shop. "Tanja called in an absolute panic, saying you were fighting a monster. And we just saw you step through some kind of portal!"

"I think the fight accounts for the mess," Dante said dryly as he closed the door.

"It's a long story." Shan sighed and turned to Dante. "Do you have a blowtorch?"

"A blowtorch?" The ex-marine shot her an incredulous look. "What for?"

"What is this thing?" Phylicia reached for the demon grimoire.

"Don't!" Shan slapped her mother-in-law's hand away from the book. "I'm sorry, but it's too dangerous for you or any witch to touch. And it's why I need a blowtorch. I've got to destroy the grimoire. It's from another dimension."

"What about the acetylene torch in my studio?" Dante asked.

"That should work." Shan nodded.

"I want to know—" The bells on the store door interrupted Phylicia.

"You're back!" Grandmother Wong said cheerfully as she stepped into Morrigan's Cauldron. "Where did the Noktiti take you?"

"What's a Noktiti?" Phylicia's attention shifted from Grandmother to Shan and back.

"They're a silicon-based lifeform that wanted to use you as a pathway to invade our world," Shan said. "That grimoire is made out of them, and the longer I wait to destroy the damn thing, the more likely it is we're looking at a full-blown invasion. Please, check on the girls, and I promise to explain everything when Dante and I get back."

"Here, Shan." Grandmother unwound the crimson silk scarf she wore tucked beneath her coat. "Wrap the grimoire in this to protect Dante. You will have to burn the scarf, too. I'll stay with Phylicia and the children until you and Dante return."

Shan nodded as she accepted the silk. She'd learned to heed her grandmother's words long before she knew her grandmother's true identity. Once the grimoire was covered, Shan followed Dante out of the store and across the street to his and Phylicia's minivan.

Once they climbed into the vehicle, Dante cranked up the heat since Shan hadn't wasted the time by running upstairs for her coat. He checked traffic before he pulled away from the curb. At this time of night, the streets of Greenwich Village were fairly quiet.

Jamal had inherited Tom's gym when he died. Dante had helped Jamal manage the gym, but once he had been selected as a civilian specialist by NASA, Dante took over full-time. He'd also converted the apartment on the second floor into a studio for his metal art with Jamal's permission. Surprisingly, the ex-marine remained silent during the entire ride to the gym.

After he parked his minivan by the stairs leading up to the studio, Shan finally said, "Aren't you even going to ask?"

"I found out the hard way that weird shit happens around my wife and her family." Dante shrugged. "I go with the flow. If something's important like destroying that book you got, you'll tell me."

Together, they exited the minivan. Shan could have sworn she heard whispering as they climbed the steps. The grimoire emitted a piercing sound, almost like a scream, when they entered the studio itself.

Phylicia had cleaned the place, physically and psychically, upstairs and down, after they removed Tom's belongings. She had also painted warding symbols on the walls, ceiling and floor via her murals. No one would notice the symbols unless they knew what they were looking for.

"Here." Dante grabbed a huge steel bucket sitting on the floor and placed it on a couple of stacked ceramic floor tiles. "This should work. Let me grab the fire extinguisher."

"No." Aisha and Anthea's stories about the effects of water on demons flashed through Shan's brain. "We need water and salt."

"Witch stuff. Gotcha." Dante retreated to the kitchenette and pulled a canister of salt from the cupboard.

Shan laid the silk-covered grimoire in the steel bucket. She fingered the hilt of her knife while she considered her options. She couldn't risk Lexi. Her fingers paused. The explosive reaction between Lexi and Anthea's spell. What if it also happened between goddess and demon magic?

Before she could think twice about it, Shan drew her copper knife and plunged it into the book. The energy release wasn't as bad as it had been in Otherwhere, but it still knocked her on her ass. The grimoire let loose a bloodcurdling scream.

"What the hell?" Dante looked at her like she was crazy.

She climbed to her feet and peered inside the bucket. The copper blade had twisted, and the leather covering the handle was charred. Silicon gel oozed from where the knife penetrated the cover. She looked up at Dante.

"I had to make sure."

He merely nodded.

Shan donned his helmet and gloves. They were way too large, but they'd have to do. She ignited the acetylene and went to work.

An hour later, Shan settled back against the passenger seat of the minivan. She needed a shower to get rid of the soot covering her face, hands, and hair. The last thing she wanted was undead demon bits in her bed.

After she burned the grimoire to ash, Dante had filled the bucket half way with water and poured the entire carton of salt into the muck. He stirred everything for good measure.

"What should I do with the demon porridge in the morning after it's cooled?" he asked from the driver seat as they headed back to Morrigan's Cauldron.

"Double bag the bucket and everything before you throw it in the dumpster." She yawned before she added, "I'll buy you a new bucket and a few cartons of salt."

"Don't sweat it, Shan."

She glanced at her watch. It was still set to the time in Sam's California. Damn, she'd been awake almost twenty-four hours.

She leaned back against the headrest again—

—and Dante shook her. "Shan, you're home."

"What?" She blinked a few times and inhaled deeply. The sweet scents of vanilla and chocolate complemented the rich smell of fresh roasted coffee in the minivan. "Where'd the coffee come from?"

"You slept through my pit stop at the bake shop." His white teeth practically glowed against his dark skin under the street lights. "You grab the boxes. I've got the drinks."

Shan opened the passenger door and eased out of her seat. Her muscles reminded her of their trek through the fae lands and the alien desert. She slid open the side door and grabbed the two pink boxes.

What the hell was Dante thinking? Was he planning on leaving Tanja and Livvy with her for Samhain after hyping them up with sugar?

Grandmother waited for them at the main door. She held it open for them. "Did you destroyed the cursed object?"

"Yes, ma'am," Shan replied.

Grandmother poked Dante. "Did you bring me chai tea?"

"Yes, ma'am." He grinned at Grandmother as he handed it to her.

"Get upstairs," she commanded. "I'll lock up."

Fatigue plucked every fiber of Shan's being as she climbed the stairs to the loft. The girls screeched when Shan appeared. Thankfully, Phylicia retrieved the two boxes of doughnuts while two nine-year-olds and an Irish wolfhound surrounded her with hugs and licks.

"Cu Chulainn, no!" Shan commanded. "I've demon ash all over me!"

Tanja and Livvy jumped away from Shan.

"You've got what on you?" Tanja demanded.

"Is that what you were fighting downstairs?" Livvy's big blue eyes widened.

"Yes, let me get cleaned up and I'll tell you everything." Except Shan had an entourage to the bathroom. It showed how scared the girls were if they were ignoring the doughnuts.

"Girls, let Shan pee in peace," Phylicia shouted.

They giggled and ran out of the bathroom.

"You, too, Cu Chulainn." Shan pointed at the door. The dog gave her pitiful look before he trotted after Tanja and Livvy.

Shan washed up and pulled on a t-shirt and yoga pants. After she returned to the living room and grabbed her mocha and a double chocolate doughnut with sprinkles, she told the whole story, starting with the strange woman with the demon grimoire. The scariest part was the hard look on Grandmother's face as Shan weaved her tale.

"Phylicia, Dante, why don't you go home and get some sleep before your sabbat tonight?" Grandmother said. "Shan and the girls need their rest, too. I'll open the shop for you."

"But the girls—" Phylicia's protest was interrupted by a loud snore from Livvy. The girl's head hung over the arm of the couch.

Tanja was curled up on the bean bag, also sound asleep.

"But this sorceress who tried to trap me and the girls with that demon grimoire—" Phylicia started more softly.

"I'll take care of her before Adrian arrives," Grandmother answered. "He was planning to cover the store this afternoon, no? And if something happens, I have a warrior to protect me." She reached over and patted Shan's knee.

Phylicia let out a deep breath. "All right, my lady. I will do as you say." It was one of the rare times Phylicia acknowledged who and what Grandmother was.

Shan?

She jerked awake at Grandmother's voice and sat up. "What?" Cu Chulainn raised his head and blinked sleepily at her from the foot of her bed.

The sorceress is coming. I thought you might enjoy being here when she arrives.

Hearing Grandmother's voice in her head was weird, but not unexpected after the last few days on other worlds. Shan had gone to bed in her exercise clothes. Maybe she knew deep down Grandmother would call for her.

I'm coming.

Cu Chulainn blinked sleepily while Shan pulled on her running shoes. She retrieved Lexi from the closet and headed for the living room. Both Tanja and Livvy were still sound asleep on the couch and chair cushions on the floor.

"Stay and watch the girls," Shan whispered to the wolfhound. He promptly sat next to the sleeping children, but his posture remained alert.

Surprisingly, Lexie remained quiet as Shan crept down the stairs to the storeroom. Nag champa incense filled the air. Voices came from the store itself.

"There is no grimoire here," Grandmother said calmly while Shan approached the bead curtain.

"I want my property back!" someone screeched.

Shan stepped through the curtain. Yep, it was definitely the white woman from—well, last night in local time.

"I burned it," Shan said.

The woman stared at her aghast before fury filled her face. "I'll sue you!"

"You will do nothing because you are nothing but a *zhi ren*," Grandmother stated. "A bit of magic to do your master's bidding. And you will burn just like the damnable tome with which you tried to entrap my friend and tried to harm my granddaughter."

Fear filled the woman's face. She whirled and ran for the door, but it refused to budge no matter how hard she yanked on it. The bells jangled an angry tone.

Grandmother pulled the smoldering incense stick from its holder, blew on the tip, and flung the stick at the woman.

Her scream was cut short by a flash of flame. Ash drifted to settle on the mat by the door.

Shan stepped closer to Grandmother. "If she was only a *zhi ren*, a servant, then the Noktiti are in contact with her master."

"Her master is no longer a problem." Grandmother smiled, and for an instant, Shan saw her true face. "He burned with his *zhi ren*."

"Are you ever going to teach me some of your tricks?" Shan asked.

"I never thought you would ask." Pride beamed from Grandmother. "But first, would you vacuum up that dust? I don't want to leave Phylicia and Adrian's store untidy."

Shan grinned back. For once, she didn't mind cleaning up someone else's mess.

CHAPTER 37

On the count of three, Aisha stepped through the mirror. The vertigo wasn't as bad as the Noktitis' portal or Sam's teleportation. She took a deep breath and opened her mouth to contact Sparx and Nix through her repaired comm—

Only to be tackled at superspeed.

"What the hell?" she yelled.

Rey paused in midair, his arms wrapped around her. "Ghost Owl, is it really you?"

His choice of words meant law enforcement was listening in on comms.

"Yeah, Black Falcon, it's me." She laughed shakily. "Boy, do I have a story to tell you."

Her husband leaned his visor against hers. "I'm just glad I found you."

"Uh, guys," Nix said. "When the police sniper took out that woman in the park, all the monsters popped out of existence."

"There were more?" Shock filled Aisha.

"Yeah," Rey said.

"What woman?" Aisha demanded.

The comm crackled before Canyon Pointe's chief of police Lloyd Harrison said, "There was a woman in the park, speaking the same language as those creatures. She had a strange book—"

Panic ripped through Aisha. "Chief, don't touch that book! Don't let anyone touch it! It can control the mind of whoever touches it!"

"Roger that, Ghost Owl," Harrison said. Thank goodness, Anthea and Shan had told her about how the Noktiti infiltrated their worlds. Even better, the chief took her word, but that might not stop some cowboy on the force from doing something stupid in the meantime.

Rey released her and they both flew back down to Allen George Memorial Park. On the ground, Sparx, Nix, and Cobblestone surrounded the body and the grimoire near the center of the park. Cops cordoned off the area behind the superheroes.

Aisha landed between Sparx and Cobblestone, but the body on the ground consumed her attention. The dead woman had been Latinx, possibly Mexican-American from her sugar skull earrings. Strands of white stood out in her coal-dark hair. She wore jeans, a red and black striped sweater, and orthopedic shoes. Aisha tried very hard to ignore the blood and bits of flesh and bone in the grass. But the most important thing was the grimoire lay beside the corpse.

Chief Harrison strode over to Aisha. "Glad you made it back from wherever these bastards sent you, Ghost Owl." He gestured at the body. "I hate giving this kind order, but she kept opening portals, and the monsters—"

"Even with the extra help, Nix and I were overwhelmed," Sparx murmured.

Captain Mojave landed on the other side of Cobblestone. Blue Racer suddenly appeared next to Nix. Shadowstar helped a limping Silver Shield over to their group.

Aisha swallowed hard. It was rare for all of Canyon Pointe's superheroes to show up in one place. That told her just how bad things became after she got pulled into the Noktiti portal.

"One of us would have had to kill her to stop her." She faced the chief.

"By using that damned book, she was no longer human. Your officer in SWAT should be commended."

"Speaking of the book—" He waved at the tome.

"Sparx?" Aisha looked at her friend.

"Uh, do we remove the body first?" Sparx pointed at the dead woman. "They're close enough together I'll barbeque her when I blast the book."

Aisha sucked in a deep breath and released it. "We need to destroy them both to prevent those monsters from coming back."

"But our investigation—" Chief Harrison started.

"If Ghost Owl says destroy both the corpse and the book, then we destroy both of them."

Aisha turned at the deep voice behind her. Special Agent Wilbur Nesmith of the National Superhero Bureau approached them. As usual, he wore a navy suit with a matching tie, but his team trailing after him all wore khakis and black NSB windbreakers.

"Special Agent Nesmith." She nodded.

"How much of a radius do you need, Sparx?" Nesmith asked.

She blew out a deep breath. "I'd feel better if everyone was out of the park." She smirked. "Last thing I want is to accidentally fry your pacemaker, Wilbur."

For the first time since Aisha met him, Nesmith looked emotionally uncomfortable. "Thank you for your concern," he muttered.

"Black Falcon, Ghost Owl, can you give me some air surveillance?" Sparx said. "I want everything double-checked before I cut loose."

"Leaving you here alone with that book from hell ain't smart," Cobblestone rumbled.

"I'll stay here with her," Silver Shield said. "I'm the only one who can."

Aisha didn't like it, but Silver Shield was right. Sparx couldn't hurt Aisha or Rey, but they didn't need her to destroy their supersuits in public.

It took about five minutes to get the Canyon Pointe first responders and the NSB out of the park. Rey and Aisha hovered over Sparx and Silver Shield. The other five supers swept the park one last time to make sure no humans were within the grounds.

Once everyone reached the checkpoints, Aisha called out over her comm, "Fire in the hole."

Her visor darkened to protect her sight from the twin bolts of lightning that lit up the park. Silver Shield's force field held up against Sparx's raw power. Too bad, Aisha couldn't bring Anthea here for a few lessons. Sparx could probably give Sam's friend Phil a run for her money.

Black smoke rose from the corpse. However, Sparx zapped both the body and the demon grimoire twice more before she was satisfied with the pile of glowing embers.

Aisha landed beside her friend. "Sparx, I think the book's toast."

"Just wanted to make sure—" Sparx's eyes rolled to the back of her head. Aisha caught her friend as she started to go down.

"Sparx!"

"I need to lie down," Sparx mumbled. "So tired."

"Paramedics!" Chief Harrison and Special Agent Nesmith shouted at the same time.

"No." Sparx waved weakly while Aisha lowered her to the ground. "Just need a nap and electrolytes."

"And I need some ice on my ankle," Silver Shield said as Shadowstar helped her upright. "Can we postpone the post-battle briefing, Special Agent Nesmith?"

While the NSB agent protested, Aisha's suit computer flashed a message on her visor—"Private channel 4." She switch her comm system to the alternate frequency. "Yes?"

"Is it all right if I suggest our loft?" Rey asked.

She chuckled. "Not a bad idea, but give us some time. It'll give Serena a chance to check Silver Shield's injury before Nesmith arrives."

Both Aisha and Rey switched back to the first responder's channel.

"Let's meet at the Hawk's Nest in an hour," he said. "That'll give Sparx and Silver Shield time to rest, get rehydrated, and be treated for their injuries. Is that acceptable, Special Agent Nesmith?"

The head of the Canyon Pointe NSB office glared at each of the supers in turn before he snapped, "Fine."

Aisha and her law partners let the supers use their bathrooms in their apartments in the Lechuza Building to shower and change clothes. While everyone else cleaned up, Serena checked Sparx and Silver Shield's respective conditions.

Sparx lay on Aisha and Rey's couch, sipping a sports drink through a straw while the IV Serena inserted in Sparx's hand fed her potassium. Silver Shield sat on the matching love seat with her sprained ankle wrapped in a frozen gel bag and propped up on the ottoman.

Meanwhile, Mitch brought his toys to the two ladies, solemnly stating that playing would make them feel better. When they politely declined, Mitch said, "Do you want Mommy or Daddy to read you a story? That always makes me feel better."

Rey picked up their son and swung him through the air, which elicited giggles. Aisha's heart skipped a beat. She been so scared she'd never see them again. Damn, it was good to be home.

The intercom buzzed. Rey and Mitch paused in playing airplane while Aisha walked over to the device and pressed the button to answer. "Yes?"

"Harri and the rest are back with the food," their IT guru Arthur reported. "Both Agent Nesmith and Chief Harrison are with them."

Aisha wanted to groan, but from the couch, Spark said, "Are they icing out Special Agent Consuelo?"

Serena started cleaning up her supplies. As an unregistered super, she needed to get out of here before the law enforcement officers arrived.

"I don't think so, ma'am," Arthur replied. "Special Agent Consuelo just pulled into our garage."

Of course, the head of Canyon Pointe's FBI office was here. She, along with Nesmith and Harrison had worked too hard to clean up the corruption in their respective departments over the last few years.

"Thanks, Arthur." Aisha turned to Mitch.

"I don't wanna go down to Patty's," he whined. "Can't I play with Diego?"

Aisha pursed her lips for a moment. She hated imposing on Harri and Tim's foster son, but she didn't have time for a preschooler meltdown.

"We'll ask, but if he says no, you need to go down to Patty's apartment."

"Deal." Mitch held up his palm, and they high-fived to seal the agreement.

She walked him across the hallway and knocked on the door to Harri's loft. Diego slid open the door.

"Hey, Aisha! Hey, little dude!" He held up his palm, and Mitch high-fived him.

"I'm sorry, but—" she started.

"No worries." Diego grinned. "That's why I didn't go with Harri on the food run. Come on in, little dude."

"Can you read me some more of your dragon book?" Mitch whispered.

"Dragon book?" Aisha lifted her eyebrow.

"It's something I'm writing," Diego said. "It's very G. I promise." He crossed himself.

"All right." Aisha couldn't help chuckling. "I'll bring over some food for you guys."

Diego lowered his voice. "Would you mind slipping us some hot dogs? Between Tim's low-carb cooking and Harri's run to Nolan's—"

Aisha nodded. "I can even sneak over some buns and mac and cheese as long as you don't mind Rey added broccoli."

"As long as he added his usual amount of cheese." Diego held up his hands and spread his fingers.

"Thanks." Aisha breathed a sigh of relief. "I owe you."

"Yes, you do," the teen teased.

Aisha turned away from Harri's apartment. Did her law partner know about her foster son's writing? She'd have to ask after their guests left.

An hour later, everyone had pretty much forgotten their steaks, potatoes, and veggies on their plates at Aisha and Rey's extended dining table. They all stared at her.

"Y-you've been gone for days?" Rey blinked in surprise.

Aisha shrugged. "Just from my point-of-view. It's the theory of relativity. It took Sam a few days to get me, Shan, and Anthea to the Fates to ask for their help to get us home."

"I'm still trying to wrap my head around a goddess of death named Sam," Harri murmured.

Special Agent Nesmith leaned his elbows on the table. "Could these Noktiti things come back?"

"They might," Aisha admitted. "But if Anthea succeeds, we won't see them again." She reached under the table and squeezed Rey's hand.

He smiled back at her.

She realized it didn't matter if anyone believed her wild story or not. She was home. And that was all she cared about.

CHAPTER 38

Sam stepped through the Fates' mirror and into her own living room.

And for the first time ever, Cara Lannigan lowered her sidearm instead of shooting her.

"Miracles do happen." Sarcasm dripped from Sam's voice.

Cara's cheeks turned beet red. "Maybe if you used a door once in a while, I wouldn't draw my gun."

"How was your consultation with the Fates?"

At her husband's delightful British accent, Sam whirled and threw herself into his arms. "Duncan! You're home!"

"And?" he prompted as he hugged her in return.

"Everyone's home safe and sound." She grinned up at him. "Who tattled? Phil or Connie?"

Duncan chuckled. "They both did, though Bebe was the one who called me first."

"That little snitch." Sam grimaced.

"In all fairness, she would not have if you had not teleported your foundlings into her home instead of ours." Duncan deliberately tweaked Sam's nose.

"The pack master did ask if we need to prepare for a possible invasion by these so-called demons," Cara said.

Sam turned to face Cara. "Tell John to stand down for now. I'll see if

I can dig some more information out of the Grey Ladies during the next poker game."

"The Fates are coming here?" Color drained from Duncan's face. "Are you sure that is wise, Samantha?"

She shrugged. "They asked to join. It would have been rude to say no, especially after they helped some friends of mine to return to their home worlds."

"The death goddesses are one thing." Duncan stared at her like she'd grown another head. "The Fates are something else altogether."

"Take it easy, sweetie." She patted his chest. "It's never a bad thing to have extra friends."

"But your extra friends usually come with a price."

"So did yours," Sam shot back. "You didn't hear me bitching."

Duncan scowled at her. "Actually, you did. More than once."

"How about giving all the staff the day off for my next girls' night?" she asked. "And you can take the kids to Tiffany and Ptolemy's for pizza and movies."

"Very well." He blew out the exasperated sigh he always did when he was annoyed with her decision. "I shall entertain the children while you . . . network."

"I'm so glad you get me." Sam hugged him again and added a kiss for good measure.

And she really was. No sarcasm. No jokes.

Because she couldn't imagine her life without Duncan and her children.

Turn the page, and check out the first chapter of volume one in my latest series, *Soccer Moms of the Apocalypse!*

PESTILENCE IN PUMPKIN SPICE
Excerpt © 2022, Suzan Harden

Penny Hudson guided her white minivan into one of the five free parking slots in the Oakfield Recreational Center lot while she tried to ignore the pain behind her eye sockets that had plagued her since lunchtime. The trees around the soccer fields had turned from green to gold and orange since last week's games. Brilliant leaves gleamed against the dark clouds to the west. The falling barometric pressure from the incoming weather front was probably the cause of her headache.

It would be a race between the soccer teams finishing the last round of games for Tuesday evening and the storm threatening to put an end to the park's activities. No sooner had she put the transmission into park, her daughter Justine yanked the back door of the vehicle open, jumped out, and raced up the sidewalk toward the park gate.

And left the dang van door wide open.

"Puberty, thou art a heartless bitch," Penny muttered under her breath. Their relationship had seemed to disintegrate when Justine turned twelve this summer. The last thing she needed was a major mother-daughter meltdown in front of the snooty parents and the resulting clucks and advice.

Francine Coy-Astin could be snooty, but she was the only stay-at-home team mom who would acknowledge the existence of the three working moms. Plus, Francine's daughter Brittany was a better player than most of the boys, which meant Francine was persona non grata with the rest of the moms for having an athletic daughter, so she hung out with the other three outcasts.

The crisp fall air and the scent of burning leaves mixed with the aromas of the four coffees in the drink carrier sitting on the front passenger seat. Children's shouts and cheers followed on the wind. Penny stabbed the button to close the back door. Thank goodness, she managed to talk Gene into the top package with the power doors when they bought the van. Otherwise, she might be tempted to slam the head of their only child in the manual doors of her old mini utility vehicle.

Penny tucked her purse under the driver seat and collected the drink carrier. With the chill wind and the overcast sky, she was glad she remembered to wear her sweatshirt. She pressed the locking button on her fob. The minivan beeped, its lights flashed, and she shoved the fob into her front jeans pocket.

A brand-new minivan, one she didn't recognize, was parked near the entrance to the stands. She felt a little sorry for the owner. Courtney Lasser, the president of the Oakfield Parents Association, and the rest of her stuck-up crew would definitely mock the puke green color. She started to pass it when she spotted the gold Saint Christopher medallion hanging from the rearview mirror.

And recognized the dark-haired woman with her head leaning against the steering wheel.

Penny walked around the van and knocked on the driver side window. Dani Elante jerked her head up and wildly looked around. Penny stepped back as her friend popped open the door.

"You okay?" Penny handed the Valencia double mocha from her coffee shop to Dani.

Her friend took a deep breath of the steam that wisped from her cup. "Yeah. Nothing military school wouldn't fix."

Penny rolled her eyes. "Puberty. God's punishment for one night of fun. If it makes you feel better, Justine began breakfast with the announcement that I needed to start buying her tampons."

Dani winced. "In front of Gene's dad?"

"Yep." Brown and yellow leaves crunched beneath their feet as they walked up the sidewalk to the entrance of the soccer field. They both paid the token fee to attend the game. Courtney's second in command Helen Chow made a point of glaring at their cups from Penny's coffee shop while she took their cash. Penny and Dani made an equal point of ignoring her. Cream, sugar, and a bottle of antacid couldn't redeem the burnt sludge served at the league's refreshment stand.

They started walking toward the aluminum torture devices the Oakfield Park Service referred to as audience stands. "I then got a lecture from Edward about how it would be my fault if Justine got knocked up before she graduated because I was too permissive with my hippy lifestyle."

"Maybe it's time to drop your bomb," Dani said.

Penny shook her head. "If he knew I knew he had an affair while Laura was in hospice, it would kill him."

"I'd do it," Dani said.

Penny chuckled. "No, you wouldn't. You are the last person in the world who would hurt someone."

"What is his problem with you?"

"According to him, I'm un-American for dressing up a plain cup of joe."

Dani laughed. "But you're the epitome of capitalism."

"Speaking of capitalism, I heard that developer Rimmon bought the Spenser Building downtown and plans to tear it down."

"Yeah, the Oakfield Historic Association is throwing a hissy fit, but that place is a death trap." Dani shook her head. "If the association really cared, they should have raised the funds to restore it before the roof caved in."

Penny climbed behind Dani to the top of the stands where Wila Ardale had claimed their usual spot, well away from the rest of the Tiger Shark team parents.

"I see you joined the minivan brigade." Wila's teeth flashed against her dark skin.

"I didn't have a choice," Dani grumbled.

Penny snorted as she handed Wila her white chocolate mocha. "Yes, you did. Chuck was being a cheap ass, and you should have called him on it."

Dani bristled at the criticism of her father. "It's a temporary vehicle until I can save up for another pickup."

Penny tilted her head. "His idea of temporary involved you working at the insurance company for just a year after you gave birth so you had experience on your resume."

Dani winced at that remark. "Marty needs the help."

Penny snorted a second time. "And every time you try to quit to finish your degree, your dad lays a million reasons on you not to leave, and your brother gives you a raise. When are you going to start living your own life?"

"I like working there." Dani's statement sounded half-hearted. "Besides you're the one saying I didn't do my fair share of carpooling, so a minivan makes sense."

"At least mine's not vomit green," Penny mumbled into her cup.

Wila leaned over and gave Dani a knowing wink. "Don't let her rattle your cage. She's just saying that because she keeps losing her minivan in the sea of white ones at the mall."

Penny scowled at Wila. "At least I don't need to make a spectacle of myself with that bright red atrocity you choose."

Dani sighed. "I miss my pick-up."

"You're damn lucky that drunk driver didn't kill you. A truck can be replaced." Penny took another sip of her coffee. "But you and Mark can't." She immediately regretted her words at Dani's bleak expression. "I'm sorry. I shouldn't have—"

Dani waved her free hand and sniffed back the threatening tears. "It's not like I haven't been thinking the same thing. Wila can tell you what a mess I was at the scene."

"Actually, I was more worried Sergeant Park would end up arresting you for murder the way you were beating on the other driver." Wila peered over her shoulder at Dani's new minivan. "Let me guess. Chuck took the best deal on Neal's lot."

Penny appreciated Wila changing the subject. She'd first met Dani shortly after her husband Heath had been killed by another drunk driver. Dani had sat in Penny's café, staring blankly at the wall while her plain black coffee grew cold. The two women had bonded while Dani tried to put her life back together.

Francine plopped down next to Dani. "Neal told him he could order a pick-up in whatever color you guys wanted." Her hot pink manicure contrasted with the olive green liquid in her reusable drink bottle. She must still be on her juicing cleanse.

Penny handed Francine her double French vanilla espresso. She popped off the lid of the coffee cup, unscrewed the cap on her bottle, and poured the espresso into the juice.

"Why can't you drink coffee like a normal person?" Penny shuddered in disgust.

Francine screwed the cap back on and shook her bottle to mix the contents. "Because I care about my health and my family's health." She took a drink of her noxious-looking mixture. "It's why none of my family caught that crud you brought back from your Florida vacation."

"Yeah." Penny rolled her eyes. "I specifically brought back the plague just to infect the entire town."

She sipped her pumpkin spice latte. The caffeine helped her headache, but the wind picked up, driving dead leaves across the field and sucking away the little warmth she got from the hot milk and espresso. The coaches gathered their teams for their pre-game huddle. Justine's face puckered into a pout when Coach Cordero named the starters who ran out to take their positions.

Justine stomped back to the bench and dropped on it dramatically. At least, the coach had called and discussed the fight between her daughter and Kenny Lasser. Cordero said he would have benched Justine for taunting Kenny at Thursday's practice regardless of any threats from Courtney. He refused to reward poor player behavior. His even-handedness when it came to the players was one of the reasons Penny loved him as a coach.

The referee placed the ball on the field between the two teams and raised his whistle to his lips. A horrendous boom behind Penny drowned out the referee and his whistle.

Everyone looked behind the bleachers in time to see a jagged fork of lightning split the boiling black clouds rushing in from the west. So much for the game beating the storm. Another crack of thunder pierced Penny's ears. Both the refs and the coaches started blowing their whistles and yelling for everybody to clear the fields.

Francine rolled her eyes. "And I skipped hot yoga for this."

"If you want to stay up in these aluminum stands and be electrocuted, fine!" Wila stood. "But get your scrawny ass out of my fu—" A third crack of thunder drowned the rest of her insult.

A blast of cold wind with even colder splatters of rain obviously spurred Francine more than Wila's insults. She jumped up and headed down the steps. Heaven forbid the weather ruined her perfectly highlighted blond coif.

Dani hung on to her coffee for dear life as she scrambled down as well. Penny followed, praying the clouds didn't cut loose before she reached the bottom. The last thing she needed was to slip on wet aluminum, tumble down the bleachers, and break her neck. She stepped onto the concrete, and heavier drops splashed on the slab that anchored the metal.

"Come on, Mom," Justine yelled. She took off for their vehicle, not pausing to make sure Penny followed, Dani's son Mark right behind her.

"Nice to know they're concerned about our welfare," Dani muttered.

Penny held up her keys and jangled them. "It's not like they can get in without us." They laughed and jogged after the kids.

"See you at girls' night!" Wila waved before heading in the direction of her painfully bright red ride with her son Derek.

Francine said nothing. She was too focused on grabbing Brittany and racing for their own vehicle.

Justine shrieked as the heavy drops turned into a deluge and yanked futilely at the back door latch. On the run herself, Penny hit the button on her key fob to unlock her minivan's doors. They were both soaked to the skin when they dove into the van.

"This just sucks!" Justine leaned over the center console to shout in Penny's ear. "Look at my hair! I spent an hour straightening it, and now, it's going to frizz!"

Penny rubbed her temples with her fingertips. The headache she'd chalked up to the incoming storm grew worse. "Please don't yell at me."

"I'm yelling because-because-b—" Justine jerked back. "Oh, my god! Get the door open! I'm gonna be—"

Penny's fingers couldn't move fast enough. Despite Justine's effort to turn aside, vomit shot all over the minivan's center console and the right sleeve of Penny's sweatshirt.

Including her unfinished pumpkin spice latte in the minivan's cup holder.

Acknowledgments

As always, much love and appreciation to Elaina Lee and JW Manus for their wonderful design work,

More love to Darling Husband and Princess Bella,

And finally to everyone out there who writes fan fiction, don't stop learning!

About the Author

Suzan Harden transitioned from writing information technology manuals for companies and legal articles for a law enforcement magazine to her first love, fantasy and science fiction in all their forms. She's the author of the Bloodlines, the 888-555-HERO, and the Justice series.

www.ingramcontent.com/pod-product-compliance
Lightning Source LLC
Chambersburg PA
CBHW071528120726
47907CB00013B/1255